WINE, CHEESE… AND DAGGERS

(ARE BACK IN STYLE)

MARILYN SMITH PORTER

Marilyn S. Porter
MarilynSPorter1217@gmail.com
Paperback ISBN: 979-8992913811
Editor: Rachael Horn
Cover Designed By: Victoria Lauren Bryan

TABLE OF CONTENTS

A VIEW TO A LIE

Police Headquarters, New York City, February 1979

It was early evening, 5 o'clock, when the call came into the 19th Precinct, Manhattan. It was the first moments of a case that the Upper East Side station would never forget. A case that would be discussed for years to come. No one saw it coming. No one could have guessed. And yet, it all started out so simply.

* * *

It had been a busy Thursday in the robbery division. Seems the thieves were enjoying a surge in activity in the city that never sleeps. You could almost smell the crime pouring out from the cold, muggy sewers. The precinct was nearly empty at the end of the day. So, as it happened, Chief Patton knew he was going to have to send his number one homicide detective on a robbery call. Not always a good idea, but crime had no respect for rank. Ever. After putting it off as long as he could, the Chief summoned Detective Tracy into his sterile office. He imparted the basic information to the detective who was considered the best of the best in homicide, and the one they called "the Rock Hudson of the NYPD." Standing a notch above 6-feet with dark hair graying at the temples and a rugged face with a jaw that could cut paper, at age 47 Nick Tracy was still well-proportioned with no visible signs of neglect; that included his mind which was razor sharp. Some of his fellow detectives often remarked that he resembled his cartoon "namesake"; the one in the yellow trench coat, the deeply creased fedora and the futuristic two-way radio on his wrist. But Detective Tracy was much more than a mere funny paper hero. And that was a fact that someone was about to discover the hard way.

"I've got a robbery, Nick," Chief Patton began. "And I know what you're thinking. But I need you. I'm giving you some assistance. Lucky for you, Tanner is still here in the building and has already volunteered to ride along. I gave him the write-up with the address and apartment number."

Detective Tracy nodded without eye contact or comment as he left the office. Chief Patton watched through his glass wall as Tracy encountered patrolman Tanner, who followed wordlessly in his footsteps out of the squad room, through the precinct door, and into the night.

After a twenty-minute ride through midtown traffic where the dimly lit streets were slick with a cold February rain, Detective Tracy and patrolman Will Tanner found themselves outside the door of an apartment on the Upper East Side. The number was barely visible in the dimly lit hallway with the burned-out light. There was no answer to their knock; silence met silence on the other side of the wooden door. Maybe they had the wrong apartment. Tracy had Tanner check the sheet.

#717. . .burglary. . .No, this was the one. The patrolman made a half-hearted suggestion.

"Well, Detective, guess we have a couple of choices here. One being you kick in the door like they do in your favorite old black and white movies, you know the ones, tough guy. Yeah, I heard about the scuffle yesterday between you and Baker. Heard he got the better of you. You're getting soft there, *Dick Tracy.*"

"Remember when I asked for your opinion, Tanner? No? Me neither." Tracy turned away from the patrolman, who smelled like cigarettes and onions. There had been a bit of a scuffle the previous day among the detectives. Tracy was well aware the problem was of his own making. His nemesis had gotten a jump on him. He had endured more than enough ribbing from his fellow detectives.

Tanner, however, must have sensed a sore spot in New York's finest. Good place for a poke. "Kid, did I ever tell you. . ."

"Yeah. In every conversation we've had over the last twenty years, Tanner. Now if you're not going to help, get out of the way."

Nick Tracy didn't much like Will Tanner. The patrolman had an old gangster look to him, like Broderick Crawford on a bad "no-shave" day. The veteran cop was just shy of 60, short, stocky, with a misplaced neck that gave him a slight slouch to one side. And even though the old guy had a weakness for Camels and breakfast pastries, he was still in pretty good shape. Word around the precinct was that Will Tanner was thinking about retirement, so Tracy decided to show some respect, even though Tanner had always called him "kid" since Tracy's initial year on the force when he had made a rookie mistake. The old cop should have let up by now, but he hadn't.

Tracy reached for the door handle. It turned easily in his hand. He flashed a grin to the cross-armed cop and then pushed the door open wider and called out. "Mr. Lorin? NYPD."

There was no response. The apartment was dark; the window shades had been pulled down tight, not letting a ray of light through. Patrolman Tanner flipped the wall switch. A clicking noise, but no light. "Why don't I go into a connecting room kid, and try the switch in there?" Tanner suggested.

Tracy agreed and held back just inside the door. He could hear Tanner swearing under his breath as he jostled his way through the dark and unfamiliar room. There were scraping noises, chairs being knocked over, table legs grating on the floor. There was also the high-pitched yap of a barking dog. Thankfully, the yap was coming from a nearby apartment. Tracy knew Tanner was a bit squeamish. He related a story to Tracy on the ride over how he had just been bitten on the leg by a stray alley mutt while out on patrol.

After a moment, warm yellow light flooded the dining room spilling into the front room where Tracy was waiting. The detective picked his way through the maze, setting furniture upright on its feet as he advanced. When he reached the patrolman, his first reaction was one of shock. "What the hell, Tanner?"

Tracy's partner looked down at his clothing. His shoes and pant legs were smeared with blood. But there was something even more disturbing in the room. Behind them, lying on the dining room rug in a pool of blood. . . was the body of a young woman

* * *

You Only Lie Twice

The body had been removed. Detective Nick Tracy looked around at the scene of the crime with seasoned eyes that had seen it all when it came to murder. Nothing about this one, in the beginning, stood out from the others. The young woman was undoubtedly killed while sitting at the dining room table. Blood splatter covered the area. It appeared that when stabbed, the woman fell to the left landing on the floor beside the table. The only thing was that she was lying at an odd angle with her body in a position that even a contortionist would find challenging. For some reason, the image bothered Tracy. It was telling him something; he was just not clear on what that "something" was.

The detective directed his crime scene crew to comb every inch of the apartment. The murder weapon, of course, was nowhere to be found. Prints were lifted from a few pieces: a glass on the table, a couple of dishes in the sink, and a second water glass that appeared to have been washed, then set aside. All in all, there wasn't much to go on. Forensics would not be happy.

The owner of the apartment house, who lived several floors above, had been summoned and now ID'd the body as a Miss Miranda Cross. Miss Cross had rented the apartment five years prior. And according to Mr. Green, she was alone in the world: her parents were gone, and she had no siblings. Without prompting, the landlord offered a bit of additional information; Miranda had kept to herself, not often leaving the apartment except for work, paid her rent on time, no loud parties, never a peep out of her, the ideal tenant.

After excusing the building owner, Tracy sent patrolman Tanner home in a squad car to change his blood-soiled uniform and shoes. Tanner went gladly. (For a tough cop, he was absolutely squeamish). Tracy was just finishing an additional sweep of the front room when Chief Patton appeared in the doorway, classic aviators atop his balding head. "You trying to drum up business, Tracy, like we don't have enough already? This is NOT the apartment number I gave Tanner. The order said 718. Not 717."

"Sorry, Chief, but it was dark out there in the hallway. Bulb out in the sconce. Tanner must have misread your chicken-scratching. Said you wrote 717."

Chief Patton perused the room with a look that bordered on disinterest. He ran a finger along the rim of the wooden chair where Miranda Cross had once been sitting. "What do you make of it, Detective? Anything jump out at you?"

Tracy shook his head. "Nothing yet. According to the apartment house owner, a Mr. Fredric Green…young woman, mid-thirties, divorced. She worked at a bookstore around the block."

"Is there a boyfriend or an ex-husband still in the picture?" Patton questioned.

Tracy consulted his notes. "Mr. Green says she rented this apartment and moved in after the ink was dry on her divorce papers. Ex-husband's name is Charles Robertson. According to Mr. Green, he lives in Pennsylvania somewhere. Miss Cross took her maiden name back when they called it quits."

"Ok, Tracy. Do what you do best. But before that, do me a favor and check in next door. . .718. . .and take a statement on the robbery that was the original call. Let me know what you have on both cases as soon as possible. And if you don't need him, I'm going to reroute patrolman Tanner to an assault over on First." With one glance over his shoulder, Chief Patton was gone.

Tracy followed his team around the apartment for one last look. There was a small balcony overlooking the city with numerous plants scattered about. Two had been knocked over; dirt littered the balcony floor. But other than the furniture Officer Tanner had replaced, there didn't seem to be anything else disturbed. No drawers pulled open with contents scattered about. Nothing. Everything neat and tidy. Except for the blood.

Tracy took one last mental picture before turning to go. He would wait for the coroner's report to fix the time of death, and the angle of what appeared to be knife wounds might tell him something about the murderer. He would have more information by that time. As for now, he had this terrible feeling, as if whoever committed this crime was not done. Everything was too pat. Almost as if it were staged. That feeling wasn't far off track. The investigative team left the victim's apartment and closed the door behind them as Detective Tracy stopped a few feet away at apartment 718. One knock summoned the occupant inside, a Mr. Max Lorin, who appeared in the doorway in a red bathrobe and a pair of scruffy slippers. After Tracy showed his badge, the small man motioned for him to come inside. Lorin then excused himself to finish a phone call and told Tracy to have a look around.

The apartment was cookie-cutter to Miranda Cross's: egg-shell-white walls, low ceilings painted in a robins' egg blue, and wood molding throughout. The furniture had been arranged in a pattern almost identical to the one next door: a couch and two easy chairs in front room, a television set in the corner, a high desk along one wall and a square table and six chairs in the dining room. The only thing different here was an upright piano in the corner and a sad little terrier lying with his head between his front paws, who was stretched out on a dirty cushion with a gnawed-up bone near his head. His dark, beady eyes were glued to the detective as he wandered around the apartment. After a moment, Tracy couldn't resist; he crossed the room to give the pooch a scratch behind the ears while he took another mental picture. As he turned his head to the left, he realized Max Lorin was standing next to him. The man had entered the room so quietly that his presence had gone unnoticed.

"I'm sorry, Detective. That was an urgent call. Only get them on rare occasions. Being a chemist there aren't many emergencies that develop over a few-hour period. But it happens. Now, I can imagine that you want to talk about the robbery."

Max Lorin was a small man, about 5'7" with "old" eyes that drooped and sagged in the corners. His hair was prematurely gray, which would lead the average man to believe that Mr. Lorin, who was a dead ringer for Wally Cox, was somewhere in his fifties, but the truth was he hadn't yet turned forty. Tracy could picture the man holding a test tube and wearing a white lab coat, but for now Max Lorin had changed into a button-down shirt and old wrinkled khakis with a faded brown belt that was on the tightest notch possible and was still too large. The excess leather hung down the front of his pants. All in all, Max Lorin was a "before" picture in G.Q. magazine.

"I don't know if I can be of much help, Detective, but I'll try." Lorin indicated a nearby seat. Tracy sat while Max plopped down next to him in what appeared to be his favorite chair. Tracy crossed his arms over his chest and stared at the small chemist.

"Let's start, sir, with you telling me what you know. The details. What was taken?"

"Not much. . .Tracy, right? Just a few papers that were sitting over here." Max Lorin rose from the chair and walked to the desk on the far wall. "Right on top of this stack."

Tracy pulled out his notepad, made an entry, and then turned back to the chemist. "I am guessing these papers are important, Mr. Lorin, or you wouldn't have reported them stolen."

"Actually, Detective, they are totally worthless."

* * *

Doctor No (Way)

Detective Tracy's head whipped around. "Maybe you had better tell me exactly what is going on here, Mr. Lorin. Or is it 'doctor'? I'm thinking you might have a PhD attached to your name somewhere. And don't leave out any parts of the story. Because I am guessing again, but I think you know who this thief is."

"No. I don't know who the thief is, Detective, but I

suspected that I might be robbed. I have developed a formula for synthetic thermal insulation. It is quite a complicated formula, not one that I can keep in my head with any sort of reasonable accuracy, thus the need to write it down."

Max paused and ran his fingers through his graying hair. "I have been working on the project, in secret, for the last three years. My company doesn't know. Not even my mother knows. Only two friends. But I made a mistake. I allowed myself to celebrate over at The Shores Bar the night after I finished the last component, although I don't know who came up with that name, as there is no "shore" anywhere within miles. I'm sure you know the place. Pretty waitresses and a lot of some alcoholic concoctions called *whiskey sours.* Anyway, I think I may have told one too many strangers that I had made a major discovery."

Suddenly, a concerned frown rippled over the chemist's face. Tracy felt his own forehead creasing in response. "You got drunk, Mr. Lorin?" The little man didn't appear to be the kind to drink himself into a stupor.

"Yes. Pretty ridiculous, huh, Detective? I'm not really that stupid, I just have bad luck when I think too much. But what was done was done. So, the other day I took a precaution. I put some papers containing a dummy formula in a manilla envelope, marked it "top secret," and then set it on my desk under a few folders. I made it appear that the envelope was being hidden." Max gestured to the desk that had contained the "top secret "envelope. Tracy got it. At least some of it.

"What is this? Like a '007' spy thing? Because you just said that the papers are worthless. That it was a dummy formula."

"Yes, Detective. I wrote the decoy formula with three separate variances that render the finished product useless. In other words, the formula that was stolen has no value."

This whole thing seemed somehow off to Tracy: mad scientists who liked to play spy-code-ring-James-Bond, was that it? Maybe a little more information. "Okay, sir, then why report the theft to the police?"

"Because I want the thief caught. I'm truly afraid. If this man was so bold as to come to my apartment, I'm not sure what he is capable of when he discovers that the formula is a fake. I feel as though I could be in danger. If you catch the thief, I will feel a lot safer. And just so you know, I went over earlier and talked to a few of your men out in the hallway. They told me about Miranda. I'm devastated."

"You were good friends with Miss Cross next door?"

"Yes. We spent a lot of our free time together. Otto over there belongs., or rather *belonged,* to Miranda. I volunteered to dog sit for a few days to see how he got along with me alone. I was scheduled to watch Otto when Miranda goes to Italy in a few months."

"So, what about Otto, sir? Wouldn't he bark if someone strange came into this apartment?"

"No, he's very friendly, Detective. I'm sure you noticed he didn't even bark at you."

"Then do you have any specific thoughts about the murder, Mr. Lorin? Do you know of anyone who would want to kill her?"

"No, I don't know anyone. And I'm guessing this wasn't a robbery gone bad. I mean, Miranda didn't have much of anything. Some costume jewelry and an alligator purse, six years old."

"How do you know that? About the alligator purse?"

"Because Detective, I gave it to her. She admired it one day in a store window while we were out. I remembered and went back later to get it for her birthday. Of course, it wasn't real 'gator. Just stamped leather. But it was nice. And expensive. Designer.”

Tracy shifted his gaze to the terrier and then back again. “I was just thinking, Mr. Lorin. . .did Miranda Cross know that your formula was written down?”

“Yes. She knew. She was one of those two people I mentioned. But if you think she might have something to do with the robbery, you’re wrong. Miranda had a key to my apartment. She could have stolen the formula anytime. But that’s it, she didn’t want to. Miranda Cross was more than just a friend, Detective. I’m not suggesting that there was anything romantic between us; I mean, look at me. I’m not exactly James Bond or Sean Connery. No, we were more like brother and sister… and call me Max.”

Tracy gave a frustrated sigh, not knowing if the chemist was telling him the truth or leaving out bits and pieces of the story. But for now, he had to take him at his word. “One last question, sir. Where were you today? You were out of the apartment. Where did you go?”

“I went to visit my sister over in Lindenhurst. I left early this morning and got back this afternoon. Why do you ask, Detective? There is no cause for suspicion.”

“Maybe not. But the city of New York pays me to find suspicion when there’s no cause.”

The little chemist nodded. He then went to answer a phone call while Tracy made a few notes. When Max Lorin returned to the room, Tracy thanked him for the information and then broke the news that there was a possibility that he might be back later for more questioning. After leaving the chemist’s apartment, Tracy made a mental evaluation of the two cases. Despite what he implied to Max Lorin, the two didn’t seem to be linked. Setting the robbery aside, his first move was going to be questioning everyone connected with Miranda Cross. Find out who had a reason to kill her. Ex-husband? Current boyfriend? Maybe even the mild-mannered little chemist next door? It was possible. Anything was possible when it came to murder.

Once back on the street, Tracy headed to his black Dodge Charger parked nearby. But he couldn't get the little chemist out of his mind. Max Lorin was so vulnerable. So unprotected. Otto was no guard dog. So, the question - was there someone out there right now who had discovered they had been duped and was out for revenge on the little man in Apartment 718? Tracy pressed his foot on the accelerator. Tomorrow, he would try to solve a murder and a robbery.

* * *

Cold Finger

Tracy's first stop the next morning was a follow-up visit to Frederic Green, the owner of the apartment house where Max Lorin was robbed and Miranda Cross was murdered. Mr. Green occupied the unit on the fourteenth floor. He was a man of approximately 60, white-haired and very tall, with an expression that had the feel of cold gray steel sitting in a freezer. But despite his hard demeanor, the apartment house owner was receptive to Tracy's visit. When Tracy walked in, Green was wearing a jogging suit and sitting in a chair with two fingers of scotch in his hand, even though it was only 9 in the morning.

"I didn't know Miranda Cross very well, Detective. I know that sounds a bit strange since she had been my tenant for over five years, but I'm sort of a recluse. I don't hang out with people. I don't go visiting friends and relatives. And I certainly don't socialize with my renters. But I make sure I am aware of all the people who come and go in my apartments."

"And what kind of people came and went into Miranda Cross's apartment?"

"That's just it. No one. She was friends with her neighbor Max Lorin and, as far, as I know he is the only one who ever walked through that door. Of course, she may have socialized away from the apartment. She did stay out, on occasion. Sometimes overnight. And she did leave every once in a while, all dolled-up for a night on the town."

Tracy was beginning to wonder if Frederic Green had a spy camera somewhere in Miranda's apartment. "You seem to know quite a lot for someone who didn't know her all that well."

"Yeah. So let me save you the trouble of asking, Detective. I keep a very close watch on all my rented apartments by relying on building gossip. I have my little birdies who like to sing."

Tracy suddenly got the picture. Undoubtedly some little old ladies on the seventh floor, who had nothing better to do, were pimping information for Frederic Green. Maybe Green even paid them. Creepy. Tracy moved on. "Okay, Mr. Green. What can you tell me? It appears Miss Cross was murdered sometime early Thursday. Did she have any visitors that day? Did she go anywhere?"

"I don't know, Detective. I left early to visit my mother in Queens. Maybe if I had been here, we could have discovered Miranda Cross's body sooner. Or I would have known that she had a visitor."

"How about Max Lorin? Did you know that his apartment was robbed?"

"I've heard. But from what I understand there wasn't anything of value taken. Knowing Max, I'm sure he reported the theft out of fear. He spooks easily, Detective. Afraid of his own shadow is how it appears. And after he heard about Miranda, I'm sure he panicked."

"Actually, he didn't know about Miss Cross when he called the police."

"Really, Detective? I just figured one followed the other," Green said over a sip of the brown liquid.

"It did, Mr. Green. But it was the other way around. The robbery was discovered first when Mr. Lorin returned home from his sister's. He then called the police. My patrolman and I happened upon Miss Cross's body when we entered the wrong apartment."

"Interesting," the steely-eyed man replied. He looked a bit unnerved by this information, which resulted in Tracy wondering what role the icy Mr. Green played. Was he really at Mom's? Why was he so surprised that the robbery was discovered before the murder?

Tracy thanked Frederic Green and left the top floor. But he didn't leave the building. Instead, he knocked on a few doors on the seventh floor until he found a little old lady willing to talk. A Miss Emily. From the angle of her door at the end of the hallway, she would have a bird's eye view of all the apartments through her peephole.

"I don't have much information, Detective. Yesterday was a bad day for me. Arthritis was giving me conniption fits. I went to my doctor for help. The old buzzard doesn't want to give me my pills early. Like I'm some kind of dope fiend or something. Nonsense!"

Tracy couldn't imagine the little pink-cheeked woman with the bright nail polish being a drug addict. "So, you didn't see anyone go into Miranda Cross's apartment? And you didn't hear anything unusual?"

"No, Detective. When I returned from the doctor, I took my medicine and went in to watch my soap operas. I'm afraid I'm going a bit deaf, so the television may have been turned up a notch too loud."

Tracy decided to check one other detail while they were on the subject. "Did Miranda Cross and Max Lorin often visit each other's apartments?"

"Oh my, yes. Almost daily. But it was always Miss Cross going into Mr. Lorin's apartment. Except on one occasion. A late-night visit by Mr. Lorin. Very unusual. A week or so ago. But there was another man with him, I believe. Or maybe the man came a bit later. . .I am forgetful, you know. But I remember, at the time, I wondered to myself if there was finally a romance blooming between Mr. Lorin and Miss Cross. Hmmm?"

"Okay, Miss Emily. Here's my card. If you think of anything else or you hear anything through the grapevine, please let me know. Especially in regard to Max Lorin's apartment. The burglar may return."

The little old lady with the missing lap (that had long been devoured by belly overhang) looked positively excited by the prospect of being asked to spy on behalf of the police. A *Jane* Bond sort of thing. Tracy could almost picture her running to the door peephole every time she heard a noise in the dark hallway.

"I will do that, Detective Tracy. I'm sure I can be of help. I'm quite observant, you know. And, by the way, I love the name. . .yours, I mean. Nick Tracy? Awfully close to Dick Tracy, huh? I bet you get this all the time, don't you?"

"Yes, ma'am. I do. And now. . ."Tracy dismissed himself from Miss Emily's grasp and left apartment 720 with its colorful wallpaper and a surprising smell of applesauce. His next stop was going to be a name given to him by the apartment owner, Frederic Green. It was the personal reference Miranda Cross had used when applying for the apartment: a character reference with a very high-end, Uptown, address.

* * *

Live and Let Lie

The Salvo apartment on West 78th Street made a great first impression. The formidable brick townhouse was surrounded by similar structures but somehow maintained its individuality. You needed a hefty amount of money to afford this kind of place. Tracy was impressed as he rang the doorbell. After showing his badge, he was led into a room to wait. When the two people came in to greet him, they were wearing matching jogging outfits. And they were holding hands. They were an attractive middle-aged couple who obviously enjoyed the catalog life that is achieved by the accumulation of wealth. And it showed big time. The male member of the duo spoke first after a brief handshake. He introduced himself as Raul Salvo.

"Detective Tracy. Thank you for calling us in advance. We had to postpone a few things, but we are glad to assist in finding Miranda's killer. What can we do to help?"

"Thank you, sir. Just a few questions. I was wondering how well you knew the deceased."

"Very well, Detective. She and her ex-husband were friends of ours up until their divorce five years ago. We maintained our friendship with Miranda and not Charles. She was a wonderful person."

"Did you see Miss Cross often?"

"Not lately. We have drifted apart. Gone our separate ways so to speak. But we exchange phone calls and Christmas cards. My wife stops in on occasion at the bookstore where Miranda worked."

Raul Salvo turned to his wife as if giving her the floor. And she snatched it. She held out a delicate, well-manicured hand with a solid gold bracelet dangling from a slim wrist.

"I'm Madeline, Detective. And I'm afraid I haven't seen Miranda in months. But I did hear through mutual friends that she was doing well. The owner of the bookstore where she works is a man by the name of White. Don't know much about him, but he might know more than I do."

Tracy tried to put his next question as delicately as possible.

"Do either of you know anyone who would want to harm Miss Cross? How about the ex? Is he capable of killing his ex-wife in anger or for any specific reason?

Both heads shook at the same time. Madeline

looked as though she might cry. But it was Raul who replied for both.

"No. I know you always turn to the spouse or ex-spouse in a case like this, but I think that's not very likely, Detective. Charles Robertson is not able, physically, to harm anyone. A car accident left him paralyzed. He's been confined to a wheelchair for over a year."

* * *

The Guy Who Loathed Me

The Manhattan Bookstore had one of those annoying bells that tinkled when the door was opened. Tracy felt the sound of the brass ringer going through his head, worsening a headache that was pounding its way through his skull, as he pushed open the door and headed straight to the counter. A large, rotund middle-aged man of Indian descent welcomed him. Tracy flashed his badge as he asked the question. "I'm looking for a Mr. White."

The Indian man smiled with large white teeth. When he opened his mouth, his accent was thick. "You have found him. What can I do for you, Detective? Is it in regards to Miranda?"

"Yes, sir. What can you tell me? And do you know anyone who would want to harm Miss Cross? Was she frightened about anything?"

"No, Detective. She was not frightened about anything. Everyone liked Miranda Cross. The only person in this world who didn't is me."

"Is there a reason, Mr. White." Tracy asked the man who was lighting a cigarette, wrapping his lips around the rolled tobacco.

"Let's just call it a 'conflict of personalities,' Detective. She was a do-gooder. Wanted to help everyone, including me. I had to return her nose. I found it in my business."

18

"Then why keep her on? Why not fire her and get someone else?"

"Because she was good at her job. People liked her. Our business is based on repeat customers. There are too many bookstores out there. Sometimes the only difference is the girl behind the counter who takes the time to find that one book in a million that someone wants. It's a rare quality."

Mr. White offered Tracy a cigarette from the red and white pack. Tracy declined. "Okay, Mr. White. Thank you for your time."

White grabbed Tracy's attention as he started for the door. "Try next door, Detective, at the ice cream shop. Miranda and Jill Masters ate lunch together."

Tracy thanked the man who was taking another drag off the cigarette. He tried to shut out the noise of the brass bell as he exited the front door. The headache was still running rampant.

* * *

The little ice cream shop next to the Manhattan Book Store was stuffed with people. The day had warmed up and ice cream sounded good. Tracy flashed his badge over the sea of heads, and Miss Jill Masters waved him back behind the counter. The young woman in her late 20s was scooping ice cream and stuffing it into cones alongside a pimply-faced kid clad in an apron and a paper hat. A sort of creamery assembly line. When there was a break in the action, Tracy asked his first question of the young lady who reminded him of Gayle Storm, with her brown hair and huge smile. "I am wondering, Miss Masters, how well you knew Miranda Cross. I understand you ate lunch together every day. Did she ever disclose to you that she feared for her life or was having trouble with anyone?"

"No, she didn't. Miranda seemed happy. She was

saving for a trip to Italy in the fall. She knew exactly where she wanted to go. Florence, Rome, Naples, the Pompeii ruins. She had these colored travel brochures that we use to look at every day. I was so shocked when Mr. White told me what happened. I cried. She was my friend."

"Do you have an opinion of Mr. White?"

There was nothing but emphasis in the young girl's answer. "I don't like him. And he doesn't like me. He didn't like Miranda either. But he needed her, so he kept her on at the shop."

"Yes, he told me."

"Really? I'm surprised he admitted it to a police officer. I don't suppose he is under suspicion, is he?"

"No."

"Too bad," Jill Master mumbled under her breath.

Suddenly, there was the beginning of a grumbling from customers waiting for their cones. The kid in the paper hat was glaring in their direction. He picked the wrong day to do such a thing. The throbbing in Tracy's head was picking up steam. He yelled out to the kid. "I'm almost finished here. . ."

"Derek," Jill Masters interjected.

"Yeah, Derek. She will be there soon. Take over for her until we're done."

Derek-with-the-paper-hat gave Tracy a disagreeable look and grabbed for the scoop as Tracy submitted his final question to Jill Masters. "Did Miranda Cross talk about her ex-husband?"

"Yes. She mentioned Charlie on occasion. Their relationship had gotten better since the accident. And there weren't any men in her life right now other than Max Lorin, and he's just a friend."

"Thank you, Miss Masters. I will stop in again if I think of any other questions. In the meantime, don't let Derek push you around, okay? He looks like a bully to me."

Jill Masters let out with a hearty laugh. Apparently, she knew something Tracy didn't. She went back to stuffing cones as the detective shouldered his way through the crowd and out the door. He needed some air. And he needed a killer with an opportunity and a motive. . .and a thief with the same.

* * *

License to Steal

Detective Tracy arrived back at his precinct, nursing his headache and a growing frustration. He had two cases, similar but not. Did he need to solve the murder of Miranda Cross first? Or the case of the Max Lorin theft? Maybe it didn't matter. Setting aside the murder case, he decided to look at the theft of the useless formula. Max Lorin had given him two names.

First was the name of his boss at the chemical plant, which was located in Long Island City just across the bridge from Manhattan, an industrial area that was close enough to the city to keep property values up. Since the boss wasn't in, he dialed another number, the other name on Max Lorin's list: his best friend. Sometimes, friends are not friends, and no one was to be counted out. Tracy made contact with the good buddy, got an address, and headed uptown.

Felix Leitner, like Max Lorin, was a young man in his thirties. When Tracy caught up with Felix, he was coming out of his apartment. From what Tracy could tell in the first five minutes, more than several degrees of difference separated the two friends. Starting with their respective apartments. Was it the bachelor pad feel or the well-stocked mini-bar? Maybe it was Felix Leitner's demeanor. Where Max Lorin was intellectual and stoic, Felix Leitner seemed to be about the social and superficial; a fun-loving kind of carefree guy who undoubtedly possessed a list of favorite haunts, the kind of haunts where a few bucks to flash around will almost guarantee that someone is leaving on your arm by the end of the night. Tracy knew some of these haunts. Especially popular was The Shores, a dimly lit destination over-flowing with girls who would gladly sit down next to you with just a promise of a drink and a few laughs.

After a minute or two of conversation, Leitner suggested a small coffee shop next to his building with outside tables. It was a quiet place with strong brew and very few trimmings. Tracy let Leitner lead the way and once they were seated comfortably, he opened with a summary of why he was inquiring into his friendship with Max Lorin. He didn't reveal the fact that the stolen papers were worthless.

"I understand you frequent the clubs around town on occasion, Mr. Leitner, so can you recall a night a few weeks ago when you were at The Shores with Max Lorin?" Tracy sat back as the waitress brought two mugs of steaming caffeine. Both men took sips.

"Yeah, Detective. I remember that night. It was the first time I had been able to drag Max out of that apartment for some fun. He is such a stick in the mud. I have to kidnap him to get him to go anywhere with me. Don't know why I try so hard except for the fact that Max Lorin is my best friend."

"So that night at The Shores. . .I understand Mr. Lorin got a bit drunk."

"Yeah. Drunk, for Max. Nothing like falling down drunk, just a bit happy. He was actually talking to women and even laughing."

"Do you know why he was so happy that night? What was he celebrating?"

"Yeah. He told me he had finished a project he had been working on. Some formula or something. I didn't listen too much. I was hitting on this really cool girl with blond hair and..."

Tracy needed to keep Felix Leitner on track, even if that meant interrupting. "What about after Max had a few beers? Was he talking more about the project?"

Felix looked disappointed, as though he wanted to continue boasting, but he jumped back on track. "Yeah. I couldn't get him to shut up. I told him women didn't want to hear about some boring chemical formula, and he needed to put a cork in it, but he didn't listen to me."

"What exactly was he saying?"

"Oh, you know, stuff like. . .'I am going to be famous, I'm going to be rich, I 've made a discovery that's going to change something-or-other, I can't remember exactly. Is this important?"

"Yeah, it might be. Who was he telling all this stuff to?"

"Everyone. He was talking loudly, like real loud. Everyone within twenty feet probably heard."

"Did you know any of these girls? Or any of the guys?"

"I'd seen some of the guys around. The women were new. But I don't think any of them were impressed with all of that stuff Max was dishing out. It was like Jell-O. You really couldn't chew it."

"Yeah, I get it. Alright, Mr. Leitner, I think that's all for now. If you think of anything that might be useful in this investigation, here's my card. Call me anytime."

Tracy finished the last bit of his coffee and then threw a dollar bill on the table. He left Felix Leitner at the café and headed back to the precinct. He thought about heading over to The Shores, but he doubted anyone there, even the bartender, would remember some indiscriminate drunk guy from two weeks before who was spouting off about a formula. He had to figure out who would be brazen enough to go after Max Lorin's project in broad daylight. How did they know he would be out of the apartment?

Were they casing the place beforehand? But most importantly, what would the thief do when he found out the papers were dummies?

Detective Tracy needed to know the answer to that last question. He didn't need another 7th- floor murder on his hands. The smart little chemist couldn't meet with any unfortunate "accident" on his watch. He called the precinct and asked to speak to the scheduling officer. "I have a change of plans, Fitz."

"I didn't know there was a plan, Detective Tracy."

"Good. Then you won't mind the change. I need a detail on one of our victims of a robbery. Guy by the name of Max Lorin. A 24/7. Tanner knows the location. He can give you the details."

* * *

For Your Lies Only

Detective Tracy checked over his notes on a Sunday morning before walking the dogs and changing the bird cage papers. Tracy had a soft heart when it came to animals. This could be the reason he now possessed a menagerie that consisted of three dogs of varying sizes that had showed up on his doorstep over the years, a stray alley cat named Lucy, two cockatoos named Bud and Lew that his neighbor had abandoned, and a couple of lizards that had escaped a pair of tires on the city street and needed a home.

While hooking up leashes, Tracy read his notes carefully. Not as much to go on as he would have liked. Taking into consideration apartment 718 and the theft of Max Lorin's papers, anyone at the bar could have overheard him bragging about his discovery. And any first-rate burglar could have broken that flimsy lock and gotten into the apartment when he wasn't home. Maybe he even left the door unlocked, the way Miranda Cross's door had

24

been unlocked when he and Tanner arrived that first night. Maybe someone at the plant where he worked got wind of his project. Maybe he let something slip. Or maybe Miranda Cross told someone she shouldn't have. She may have been his confidante, but there was no way of knowing, now, if she had kept that confidence. And taking all those facts into consideration, anyone in the city of New York could have taken those papers. So basically, he had seven million suspects. And, about the murder next door in apartment 717, no one heard anything. The little nosy neighbor lady was at her doctor's reading him the "riot act" over her pills. Max Lorin was visiting his sister. The murdered woman's ex-husband was bound to a wheelchair. Her boss didn't care for her but had no reason to kill her. Her friend confirmed that she was well-liked with no known enemies. It could have been anyone. Those seven million suspects again.

Maybe he needed to consider the possibility that the two crimes were NOT connected in any way. Like, just a strange coincidence. It was true he hadn't found any connection. Other than the fact that the two people were friends and lived next door to one another. Another consideration had to be whether there was anyone in the bar that night who also knew the Cross woman. But the only person he had found who knew both victims was Max Lorin himself.

Was he thinking that Max Lorin killed Miranda Cross and reported his papers stolen to divert attention and make himself appear a victim also? Maybe the trip to his sister's was a way to establish an alibi. He had remarked that he didn't see friends and family much. Tracy took a final drink of his coffee and hooked the last of the leashes. What exactly was he thinking? Was he starting to build a case against the little chemist? There was no evidence. And if he was wrong and someone wanted those papers bad enough, Max Lorin could be the next victim. Tracy had someone watching the apartment now, but it would be impossible to find every person in the bar that night. Max told Tracy that he had an appointment with a manufacturer the following week. If they buy, it would take that target off Max Lorin's back, and the formula will be someone else's to protect. Max had said that the real formula was hidden in his apartment in a good place. Was he lying? In Tracy's opinion, everyone in this case was lying.

* * *

Never Say Lie Again

Detective Tracy returned to work Monday morning. It was his job to keep up with his caseload. By lunchtime, he was ready for food and a little review. Over a sandwich and a soda, he allowed himself to revisit the Cross-murder-case first. On a napkin, he doodled the details:

1. *No disgruntled boyfriends, ex-husband in a wheelchair.*
2. *No known enemies.*
3. *Planning a trip to Italy sometime in the fall.*
4. *Best male friend was Max Lorin.*
5. *Killed while sitting at table. (She invited killer to table? Suggests friend or acquaintance)*
6. *Nosy neighbor lady and owner of apartment building, all out.*

Next, he did the same with the Max Lorin theft:

1. *Bragged about formula at The Shores*
2. *Stolen formula is useless. A dummy.*
3. *Lorin at his sister's house when theft and murder both   took place.*
4. *Real formula in apartment, written down somewhere.*
5. *Best friend says Max never leaves apt. except for work.*

With the last of his sandwich gone, Tracy left the deli and made a side trip to The Shores. He had been to the nightclub on several occasions. The Shores management was friendly to the boys in blue, sometimes paying for beers. But The Shores was a neighborhood hang-out. On any given Friday night, you could find anyone and everyone. . .union men, blue collar workers, some white collars too. The nightclub was closed when Tracy rapped on the door. A fuzzy-headed bartender requested to see his badge. Tracy complied. Jack Ward didn't look happy to see *anyone* at this hour.

"Ah, c'mon, cop. Can't you see we're closed?"

"And why is that a problem, Mr. Ward?'

"I've got a lot of glasses to wash. Is this really necessary?"

After Tracy planted his feet, Jack Ward stepped aside, and Tracy slipped into the black void that was The Shores after hours, following after the bartender who walked off the distance to the long oak bar where he really was washing glasses. Tracy asked the questions, and Jack Ward supplied the answers.

"Yeah, believe it or not, I remember that night, Detective. It was my wife's birthday, and she had a bunch of her lady friends in here celebrating. I couldn't pour the shots fast enough. A couple of Andrea's single friends were hanging around the bar, listening to this one guy talking about how rich he was going to be. I barely listened. I've heard it all before. What bartender hasn't? And believe me, what he was sellin' was old stuff. Sure, it's a great way to meet women, but if you can't deliver, the women catch on real fast and move on to more fertile pastures."

"What was your take?' Tracy asked, now sitting at the bar with his feet perched on the stool footrest. He did the honors of lighting the bartender's cigarette from a pack of matches at his elbow.

"It's hard to say with these nerdy guys. Their appeal can become quicksand, real fast."

"Did any of your wife's single friends hear from the guy later? After that night?"

"Not that I know of. Sylvia seemed the most interested. Sylvia French doesn't drink so she was sober. If anything had come of it, I think I would know."

"Can you get me this Sylvia French's number, Mr. Ward?"

"Yeah. Let me call my wife."

In less than a minute, the speedy bartender was back with a number. Tracy took the paper and used the pay phone at the back of the bar, near the men's room. The mouthpiece smelled like smoke with a beer chaser. He dialed the number and waited. On the third ring, a woman answered. The raspy back-room voice said she was Sylvia French. When Tracy asked about the night in question, she seemed vague. Until he reminded her, it was Andrea Ward's birthday.

"Oh, now I remember, Detective. You must be talking about the little drunk guy at the end of the bar who was bragging about some discovery he had made that was going to make him all this money. He talked about it like he was Christopher Columbus, and he had just discovered America."

Tracy chuckled. "Well, close. His name is Max Lorin, and he *has* discovered something. And I was just wondering if you gave him your phone number, or if you have seen him since that night. It's important, Miss French. So please be honest."

"Okay, yeah, so I gave him my number, so what? Is that a crime nowadays? And to answer your next question, no, he hasn't called me. Sorry, Detective."

"Okay, Miss French. Thank you for the information." Tracy paused, hoping Ms. French would open up. Sometimes when you let people talk, they say things they shouldn't. And sometimes they say things you're looking for.

"What's the deal anyway, Detective? Has he killed somebody or something?"

"No, Ms. French, he hasn't. Did he seem like the kind of guy who would do something wrong?"

"That's just it, Detective. He didn't. I wouldn't have given him my number. He was a perfect gentleman, even though he had too much to drink. That says a lot, don't you think?"

"Yes, I do. But just so you know, Max Lorin is not in any trouble. No need to bother you any further." With that, Tracy hung up the sticky receiver and went to wash his hands in the men's room, just as his pager went off. It was Chief Patton. Max Lorin needed Tracy to call at once. When he did so, the meek chemist answered on the first ring.

"Detective Tracy, one of the persons at The Shores that night is standing outside my apartment building. I know it's him. I recognized him right away. You have to come quick. I'm getting very nervous. I would swear he's staring up at my apartment."

* * *

Tomorrow Never Lies

Tracy drove as fast as he could considering the midtown traffic situation, which never seemed to get better. Arriving at Max Lorin's apartment building, he took the elevator up to the 7th floor. The door was already standing open. The small man was holding back the drapes and staring out the window to the street below as Tracy entered. When he turned around, Max Lorin had a look of fear. Tracy asked the first question. "Are you sure this person was at The Shores that night? Your friend said you had a lot to drink and . . ."

"I know it's him, Detective. I remember he had this weird look on his face. He was nursing a beer and trying to act like he wasn't listening in on my conversation. But he was."

"But how do you know this person on the street is really the one? We're seven stories up. The people look like insects from here."

Lorin shook his head. "No. I saw him when I came home for lunch. He was standing outside the building. And he's still there."

"Well, I need to get a better look. Let's go downstairs. I want you to come with me. I don't want to ID the wrong person."

The chemist agreed with a nod of his head. When the elevator deposited them on the ground floor, Tracy led the way out the back and around to the side of the building. His plan was to come around so the stalker wouldn't see them coming. When they were standing behind the outside pillar, they had a clear shot at the sidewalk across the street. Max Lorin broke out in a cold sweat as he pointed with a shaky finger at someone standing in the shadows not fifty feet away. The man was leaning up against the building, smoking a cigarette, and as Max Lorin had observed earlier, he did seem to be staring up.

"Stay here," Tracy instructed Max and went to have a better look. He didn't want to be seen. There had been many an occasion where someone had said that he had "cop" written all over his face. When Tracy came out from behind the building and crossed over, the person came into view. And when he saw who it was, and he looked back up at Max Lorrin's building. . .it came to him. That certain something that he had almost missed. That certain something that would break the case wide open and lead to the answer every cop, in every case, fears.

Lie Another Day

It had all been so simple. Why hadn't he seen it from the beginning? Now it was just a matter of getting a confession. Was that going to be easy? No. Sometimes these things fell into place inside the interrogation room, and sometimes, they backfired big time. But it was a chance that Tracy needed to take. He called The Shores and asked the bartender, Jack Ward, to come down to the station the next day. He told Jack to bring his wife's friend Sylvia French with him. His next call was to Max Lorin. The chemist was reluctant to come but relented in the end. Tracy told him it was also necessary to bring his best friend, Felix Leitner, with him. Then he called Miss Emily, his spy on the seventh floor, and told her he would send a patrol car if she was willing to come into the station. She was delighted and asked if they could turn on the siren. He was rounding up the puzzle, piece by piece. Everyone cooperated.

* * *

The next day, when they arrived, Tracy brought everyone into the interrogation meeting room and sat them down around the big table. The room was stiff with a strange energy. Everyone seemed to have eyes wide with concern and wariness. He then asked his patrolman, Will Tanner, to wait in the hallway until he called him in. This was going to be a "good cop/bad cop" tag team thing. Tanner stood outside the door at the ready, waiting for the opportunity to do his part in this little scenario. When everyone was settled in, Tracy opened with some instructions and then a small speech. "Thank you all for coming in today. You are all an integral part of the investigation into the theft of Mr. Max Lorin's formula papers and the brutal murder of Miranda Cross last Thursday . . .”

Sylvia French jumped to her feet. “Murder??? What are you talking about, Detective? On the phone, Jack said, quote, ‘an investigation into some missing papers.’ He certainly didn’t say anything about a murder.”

Jack Ward joined in. The bartender was incensed. “Yeah, Detective. What is this? You never mentioned anyone died.”

“That’s true. Because we didn’t know if the theft and the murder in the apartment next door were connected. But I’m convinced now that they are. I’m investigating two different cases that are turning out to be one.”

Jack and Sylvia, though still ill at ease, seemed to calm down enough to hear what the detective had to say next. Felix Leitner projected a look as if he wanted to speak, but it was his best friend, the chemist, who interjected with a sense of outrage.

“What are you talking about, Detective? You aren’t seriously thinking that I had anything to do with Miranda’s death because that would be ridiculous as I am clearly innocent here.”

“No, Mr. Lorin. Maybe you didn’t kill Miranda Cross, but it was because of you that she was killed. If you don’t mind, I would like to start from the beginning.”

At this, Miss Emily snickered out loud, looking thoroughly excited about all the drama going on around her. Everyone stared in her direction, but she relinquished the floor to Tracy, who suddenly had the room’s undivided attention. “Excuse me for a moment, everyone, while I bring in someone. Please stay seated.”

With that, Tracy walked over to the connecting door and asked his patrolman to step inside. It was time for the “good-cop” “bad-cop” pony show. Tracy introduced Tanner to everyone, explaining that Tanner was on the call with him when they came to the apartment house that first night to investigate the theft. Tanner gave everyone a stern nod.

Next, Tracy made his way to a chalkboard at the end of the long table. He turned the chalkboard over to reveal a drawing of the two apartments, 717 and 718, side by side and identical in layout and size. Tracy wrote Amanda Cross on 717 and Max Lorin on 718 and then turned to his guests. He was rolling the chalk over and over in his hand as Jack Ward let out a loud cough.

"I believe the thief entered the wrong apartment that Thursday. He or she had never been there before and were only using what they saw at an earlier date. . .that being the night Mr. Lorin went out celebrating and telling everyone at The Shores bar how important his discovery was. The thief heard every word. He or she followed him home and saw him go into Amanda Cross's apartment. This is all according to Miss Emily here, who was observing through her peephole."

Sylvia French coughed nervously but didn't comment. Max Lorin did. "Maybe I never told you, Detective, because I was so drunk that night, I thought Miranda might help me sober up. So, when I took that cab home, I went next door to see her first. The thief must have followed me, saw me go in, and assumed that was my apartment."

Miss Emily bobbed her head up and down. And then she cleared her throat with a resounding cough before she began. "Excuse me, but that must have been the man I saw that night in the hallway. The one I thought was *with* Mr. Lorin. Maybe he wasn't *with him.* Maybe he was only *following* him, huh, Detective?"

Tracy nodded in agreement. He looked at the chemist. "So, the day of the planned theft, he or she waited outside your building, saw you leave and then went to break into what they thought was your apartment. And there was Miranda Cross getting ready for work. Miranda must have told them that you lived next door in 718. There couldn't be any witnesses, so the thief killed her. And then broke into your apartment, Mr. Lorin, and stole the papers."

"That seems so extreme, Detective," Felix Leitner offered with a very nervous cough. "If the thief now knew that Max lived next door, why was killing necessary?"

"I don't know for sure why the thief did what he did. But I'm going to find out. See, when patrolman Tanner and I got to Miranda's apartment, we didn't realize at the time that we were in the wrong apartment. That's how we discovered Miss Cross's body."
Patrolman Tanner nodded confirmation with another stern look.

"Sounds like this whole thing has just been a case of the wrong identity, Detective," piped up little Miss Emily, who gave another troubled sigh.

Suddenly, Tracy excused himself and took Patrolman Tanner with him. They went into the connecting room with the two-way mirror. If the people in the interrogation room knew they were being watched, they didn't let on. The two policemen observed for only a moment. Then Tracy spoke. "You know, Tanner, this whole case was built on lies from the very beginning. Two lies."

The patrolman looked puzzled. He elbowed Tracy and jerked his head towards the suspects behind the two-way glass. "I don't know how you big detectives work, but. . .but, why don't we get back in there and wrap this up? What are you waiting for, Tracy?"

"I'm waiting for the thief who turned killer to tell me the truth. Do you think I have it in the right order?"

"I don't know. Why don't you get back in there and ask the killer?"

"See, Tanner. . .I am asking the killer."

No Time to Lie

Will Tanner glanced at the door. Tracy stopped him. "Don't bother walking out of here, patrolman. Just tell me. Straight."

"What are you talking about, kid?"

"I knew from the beginning this case was based on a lie, but I didn't know if it was Max Lorin who was lying or somebody else. I just didn't figure it was my own man. The first lie you told was that Chief Patton gave you orders for apartment 717. He really gave you apartment 718. I saw the original sheet in the trash can when I went back to the station. The second lie was that the light switch inside Miranda's apartment was broken. It wasn't. I tested that, too. You needed time to get into the dining room before I discovered the body. What did you do, forget something? Some form of evidence? The knife? Did you have to find it before the lights went on? Did you get the blood on your uniform so I would send you home to change?"

"You're nuts, Tracy. Do you think I'd take that kind of chance, kid?"

"Yeah, I do. Everyone knows you're on the verge of retirement. You go to The Shores a lot, don't you? You were there that night and heard Max Lorin bragging. It would have been easy just to follow him home and then go back a few days later."

"How do you know I was in the bar that night?"

"Max Lorin. When I called Fitz to put someone on Lorin, he picked you for the detail. And when Max saw you outside his apartment building the other day, he ID'd you as one of the guys at The Shores. But just to be certain I brought in the only people who could have seen you that night. . .the bartender, the sober lady Max spoke to, and Max's best friend. And for insurance, the little old lady down the hall, snooping on her neighbors who saw a man in the hallway following Max. All four coughed after you walked into the room just now. That was the signal we had agreed upon. It was to let me know that they recognized you."

"All the cops go into The Shores. Jack could have seen me at any time. And . . ."

"That's why I brought Sylvia French in. She'd never been to The Shores before."

"You don't have proof of any of this, kid."

Tracy buzzed a phone. "Bring him in" was all he said. Chief Patton opened the door and walked in with Miranda Cross's little terrier, Otto. When Otto saw Will Tanner, he began to bark furiously. The little brown yapper went crazy trying to jump from Patton's arms and take a piece out of Officer Tanner's trousers.

"This little fella was your dog bite, wasn't it? Not some stray in an alley somewhere. I bet we could match his teeth up to those nice red bite marks on your leg. He bit you either before or after you killed his owner, Miranda Cross."

Tanner scoffed at Tracy. "You think you're so smart don't you, Detective? That damn dog was in Max Lorin's apartment, not Miranda's."

"You're right, Tanner. But the thing is, I didn't forget. And the only person, other than Max Lorin, who would know that bit of information would be the person who was in both apartments that day. The person who stole the useless papers and murdered Miranda Cross."

* * *

EPILOGUE

The Lie is Not Enough

Max Lorin took the first bite of his pasta and looked up with questions in his eyes. "Okay, Detective. I'm curious. . . tell me."

"Tanner confessed everything to the Chief. He had
a friend who worked in the chemical manufacturing
business. He saw a way to make retirement a really good
idea. If he could sell your formula."

Tracy leaned back in his chair. It wasn't often that
he had the time or money for restaurants like this. Primoli
was an upscale hot spot on the Upper East side. He turned
back to his dinner partner.

". . .After you left the apartment that day, Tanner
went up to apartment 717 thinking it was your apartment,
and he would have to break in to steal the formula. To his
surprise, it was Miranda Cross's apartment. He showed her
his badge and then Miranda told Tanner that you lived next
door but that you were out. After she closed the door,
Tanner broke into 718, your apartment. Miranda heard
some noise coming from 718, so she used the key you had
given her and came next door to see why, and that's when
she discovered Tanner putting papers in his jacket. She
quieted Otto down, but not before he bit Tanner. Miranda
felt so bad she then invited the nice policeman back to her
apartment so she could tend to the dog bite. They were
sitting at the table when Tanner killed her. He then
somehow got Otto back to your apartment, and that's when
he heard Miss Emily coming home from the doctor and, in
his haste to get out, he unknowingly left the murder
weapon in Miranda Cross's apartment. He didn't realize it
until he got back to the station. When he heard the call
come in reporting the theft he volunteered to go out on the
call so he could retrieve the knife but Chief Patton told me
to go too, so when we got to the apartment house, he gave
me the wrong number and then said the light switch didn't
work. He had to get the murder weapon before the lights
came on, and I walked into the dining room. He disposed of
the knife when I sent him home to change his bloody
clothes."

Max Lorin looked up, puzzled. "And what made you suspect Tanner in the first place?"

"After you pointed out the man watching your apartment and I saw it was Tanner I thought maybe you were wrong. Tanner is kinda ordinary looking. But I went back up to take a look around Miranda Cross's apartment and then went over to ask you if Otto barked at strangers. You told me that you had never heard Otto bark, except for the time you and Miranda were messing around, wrestling, and she cried out. Then Otto barked furiously and came at you. So, it was necessary to have Otto there at the station house when we cornered Tanner."

Max Lorin nodded over another bite of pasta. He waited for Tracy to ask the big question.

"What about the formula, Max?"

"It's in the hands of the manufacturing company that purchased it. I am going to be very wealthy, Detective. Otto and I are looking for a new apartment. It's finally hit me that Miranda is gone."

"And I have to ask you, Max... where did you hide the real equation?"

"Funny about that. The night I was at The Shores, my buddy Felix was leaving with some woman, and a nice cop at the bar called a cab for me when he saw I had to much of the liquid amnesia; he said I might forget the difference between the accelerator and the brake. The cop also told me that I had been spouting off too much about the formula and that I should put out a dummy in case someone got big ideas. Whoever the cop was, he saved me. And to answer your question. . .the real formula was disguised on the sheet music propped up on the piano in the corner of my apartment. Written in code."

Tracy smiled. Then laughed out loud. "So that explains it. One day, when was there waiting for you to get off the phone, I tried to play that sheet music. It sounded horrible."

“I didn’t know you played the piano, Detective Tracy.”

“There are a lot of things you don’t know about me, Max. I’m a pretty interesting guy. Maybe you could bring Otto by my apartment sometime to meet my menagerie? Maybe stay for dinner? I’m not a bad cook.”

THE DISAPPEARANCE OF KELLY WALTON

"I am disappearing. Maybe I am already gone."
- J. Niven

Wednesday, 9:12 P.M.

An Apartment on the Upper East Side of Manhattan

Inez Walton was middle-aged, with a face that was hard to describe. And even though the 1970s decade was coming to a close, the woman's mousy brown hair was cut into a dated '60s bob, and her makeup was right out of an issue of the defunct Shindig magazine; blue lid shadow, cat eyes rimmed in black and pale pink lipstick thick, gooey. And, at that very moment, Inez was standing at her kitchen sink staring out the window to the street six floors below and talking to herself. *Have I done everything correctly? How long will it take? Did I do the right thing by telling the police? Oh, that nice Detective Tracy. Was he doing his job?*

Inez poured another cup of coffee; how many was

that now? Even though it was late and it would keep her awake for hours. But it didn't matter. She couldn't sleep anyway. Sleep was something she had done twenty-four hours ago. Not now.

The telephone rang and Inez Walton froze. *Should she answer it? Maybe it was Detective Tracy. Maybe it was someone important. Or maybe it was no one, like one of those telephone solicitors that had cropped up in the last few years, trying to sell you carpet cleaning. . .or cemetery plots. . .or vacations to exotic places. No, she wouldn't answer, wouldn't give them a chance to goad her into something she didn't want or need.*

But in the end, Inez gave in to the incessant ringing. When she answered, the party on the other end, who just happened to be her mother, was already talking. Inez quietly fought the urge to tell her mother everything. She had promised the nice, handsome police detective that she would be silent and let the events of the last few hours just fall into place and run their course. And so, she did. She kept her mouth shut and let her mom drone on about things that didn't matter and that no one wanted to hear. It was the only way to get her off the phone. Let her run out of things to say, and then it would be over. And then it was.

Inez Walton placed the receiver in its cradle and went to stare out the window once more like a good wife. *How much longer would it be? How much more could she stand?*

And then suddenly, there was the sound of a key slipping into the lock. A familiar sound. One she had heard time and time again. The key turned. The door opened and…Inez stared at the figure in the doorway. The cup from her grandmother's set of antique china slipped through her fingers and shattered on the floor into a million pieces. And then she ran into her husband's arms. "Oh, thank God, Kelly. You're okay. I knew they would let you go."

* * *

Darkness makes everything disappear.
- C. Lounsbrough

Wednesday, 3-4:00 P.M. — Five hours earlier

The 19th Precinct

Detective Nick Tracy of the NYPD stared at his notes. He was returning from a brief lunch, and what he was looking at was troubling. No tickets out of town, not by train, plane, bus, or rental car. If Kelly Walton was leaving the state on his own accord, he was leaving under an assumed name, which was very unlikely. Maybe Tracy had been wrong. It was appearing more and more like Kelly Walton's abduction was for real. Not a hoax perpetrated by Mr. Walton as a means of escaping marital bliss or an irate boss. So, viewing the case in that light, as if everything Tracy had heard and seen so far was real, then Kelly Walton was only coming home if the $10,000 ransom was paid by his wife Inez at the corner of 68th Street and Lexington in one hour. She would never see the money again, but she would have her husband back.

And paying the ransom was exactly what Tracy was about to recommend.

The Walton Apartment

Inside the apartment, Inez Walton was pacing back and forth like a caged tiger. She was thinking and not really listening to what Detective Tracy was saying.

"Inez, you can do this. It's simple. Just think of it as throwing out the trash. Wrap the money inside the newspaper like the kidnappers have asked. And then follow their instructions. I will be around the corner, out of sight. The kidnappers won't tag me as a cop. I'm dressed in casual street clothes, no suits; even my own mother wouldn't recognize me. I will keep you safe. There is a lot of sidewalk traffic on Amsterdam, so these guys are not going to try anything stupid in broad daylight."

"But what if you intercede and the kidnappers won't let Kelly go? What if they. . ."

"Please try not to worry. I am not going to do anything foolish."

Inez Walton turned away. She didn't want to cry. Not now. She took the $10,000 off of the coffee table in front of the couch and clutched it to her chest. It felt cold. What was the saying? Cold hard cash. She slipped the bundle of paper money inside the folded newspaper and turned. "Okay, Detective. I think I'm ready. It's almost 4 o'clock. Let's get this over with."

Inez and Tracy stood simultaneously. They looked into one another's eyes for only a moment. And then they both headed for the apartment door.

Lexington Avenue

Tracy stood in the late afternoon shadows around the corner from the drop sight, the Daily Racing Form held up in front of his face. He could see the trash can. The sidewalks were crowded. But as crowded as they were, Tracy knew from experience that no one would see anything. If asked later about the woman dropping the folded newspaper in the trash can, anyone within the vicinity would say they saw nothing.

Suddenly, Inez Walton came into view. She was walking quickly, like Tracy had instructed her. But not too quickly. She looked nervous, but no one seemed to give her a second glance, which was fine. Maybe the kidnappers would notice the same thing. They would realize that as scared as she was, Inez Walton was following their instructions to the letter.

The woman with the bobbed brown hair approached the trash can on the corner of 68th and Lexington as if in slow motion. She looked around. And then she made a big flourish of putting the paper right on top of the pile of trash. Then Inez Walton turned around and went back the way she came. Back to wait and see what happened next. Would the kidnappers call again? Would they want more money? Would they release Kelly Walton unharmed? It was anybody's guess. And Tracy was not good at guessing.

At just that moment, a homeless-looking man approached the trash can. He snatched the folded newspaper with the money inside in one fell swoop and stuck it in his tattered shirt. Was it possible that he was the pickup guy?

Tracy started across the street and was almost hit by a large truck whose driver had decided he couldn't wait for some jay-walking dude. Following a barrage of horn honking, Tracy finally made it across the street. He hadn't taken his eyes off the homeless man who had ducked into a side street alley. The New York police detective took the same side street. He could see the man up ahead, loping along, as he clutched the newspaper inside his shirt. Tracy picked up the pace and arrived at the man's side in a matter of seconds. He spun the man around.

"Hey, buddy. Whatcha' got there?"

The tattered man looked puzzled. "A newspaper, cop. Yeah, I can read. And I can tell you're a cop. Can smell that cop stink all over ya', even in those undercover duds. Now what do ya' want with me? I ain't done nothin' wrong, governor."

"Let's open up that paper and just make sure that what you say is true, shall we? And then I'm going to need to see some form of ID, Mr…Mr…?"

"Jagger. Mr. Mick Jagger. Bit down on my luck, mate. See, copper. . ."

"Detective."

"Oh, well pardon me, *Detective. . .*" And then the man laughed until Tracy gave a jerk on his collar.

"Open up the paper, Mick Jagger. Let's see what you've got."

Mick opened the paper. Empty. "You're too late, copper. The guy who paid me to pick up the newspaper is gone. Ducked back into that side street over there before you got here. Nice guy. Gave me a fin for my trouble. Said he knew it was gonna go for booze, but it was okay. Said I should change my life the way he has."

Tracy grabbed for the paper. He tore open the insides, page by page. Mick was telling the truth. No money. "Okay, Mr. Jagger. You are going to give me a description of this guy who paid you because I'm assuming you had never seen or spoken with him before. . .am I right?"

"Yeah. Never saw him before, governor. But I can tell you what he looked like alright."

By the time Mick was done with his description, Tracy felt sure the homeless man had just described someone that he had met in the last few days. Tracy had interviewed a parade of characters in Kelly and Inez Walton's life and one just might fit the description Mick Jagger had provided. Was it the Walton's landlord? Or their next-door neighbor in the apartment house? Or maybe Kelly Walton's ex-boss?

Tracy let Mick Jagger go, no reason to detain him; he had taken his statement. But without any evidence, fingerprints, or reliable persons (not affiliated with The Rolling Stones) to identify the kidnappers, this abduction of Kelly Walton was headed to the cold case room real fast. In his frustration, Tracy reminded himself that from now on he should stick to homicides. These abduction cases were hard to nail down and they really pissed him off.

On his way back to the station to wait for word from Inez on her husband's return, Tracy went over and

over in his mind who and what he had seen in the last few
hours. It was quite a list.

* * *

"I realize now that I wanted to disappear."
- J. Warman

Wednesday, 11:04 A.M. — Ten hours earlier

Remco Imports Office

Tracy made an official call on Mr. Karl Fischer at
Remco Imports, mid-town. He had to wait fifteen minutes
before he was called into the enormous office that housed
Mr. Fischer and his collection of Oriental knick-knacks,
which were scattered all over like a hoarder's treasure
trove. After sitting so long in the waiting room, Tracy told
Fischer he preferred to stand and stretch his legs. Fischer
suggested they stroll the warehouse; it had always helped
him uncramp. Tracy consented, as this was exactly what he
had in mind: to see that enormous warehouse. And besides,
Fischer's office was giving him "the creeps."

Glancing sideways at Karl Fischer as they strolled
to the main warehouse, Tracy got a sense of the man. Other
than the fact that he reminded him of Dustin Hoffman in
his heyday, Fischer was a nervous talker. Once he had
found out Tracy was a cop, he seemed to feel uneasy. The
random subjects he touched on felt like a stall, as if he was
trying to get his story straight before he let Tracy take the
floor. What story did he need to tidy up?

"So, Mr. Fischer, if you don't mind my interrupting
you. . .what can you tell me about Kelly Walton? I know he
is an employee of. . ."

"*Was* an employee, Detective. I had to let Walton
go a few weeks ago. He was neglecting his work. I don't
think he told anyone because Tony in accounting saw him

46

dressed in his work clothes; the man had two suits, black
and gray. . .anyway, Tony said he sees him outside the
building every morning. Like he's coming to work, just
never coming inside. I felt bad, but I couldn't keep him on.
In fact, I felt so bad that I told Tony to give Walton a
message that I wanted to see him. When he came in, I gave
him the name of a friend of mine who is looking for a
salesman in Boston. I even lined up the interview for him.
It was yesterday. I'm guessing you know Inez has called,
but I have avoided her. I know Walton hasn't told her about
getting fired, and I didn't want to lie about it."

    "I see. Now I understand why Mr. Walton was on
that train to Boston yesterday. Did he seem depressed when
he was here? Did you get a sense of anxiety?"

    "No more than usual, Detective. Walton is a bit of a
'downer' as the kids say."

    "Do you mind giving me your friend's number in
Boston? I would like to speak to him right away."

    James Fischer took Tracy back to the trinket-strewn
office and gave him a card. Then Tracy left the office
without further explanation. Tracy wondered to himself
why Kelly Walton hadn't told Inez about the firing. Why
was he hiding the fact he was unemployed from his wife?
He would have to tell her eventually. Maybe Kelly figured
if he got the new job offer in Boston it would appear that he
was quitting Remco Imports and taking a higher position.
Bettering himself. And what was the reason that Kelly's ex-
boss never asked Tracy why the police were looking into
Kelly Walton? Wasn't the man curious? According to Inez,
Kelly worked there for 13 years. Or maybe James Fischer
already knew something he shouldn't have.

    Tracy stepped into a pay phone booth in Penn
Station and called James Fischer's friend, who had given
Kelly Walton an interview yesterday in Boston. The man
told him that Walton was only there for a few minutes.
And, unfortunately, he didn't offer Kelly employment. Said

he sent Kelly to another company he knew was looking for a salesman. He said the other man had called and thanked him for sending Walton over. He gave him a job. He also told him that Walton had left his office, saying that he was checking out of the hotel and catching a train back to New York. That was all the man could offer in the way of information. Not much to go on.

Tracy ordered some coffee to go at one of the Penn Station coffee shops. And while waiting for his order, he pulled out his notebook and made a few entries. And then he stared at what he had just written and what he knew from the last sixteen hours.

1. *Kelly Walton went missing on his way home from Boston.*
2. *Kelly Walton was kidnapped sometime yesterday after the interviews*
3. *Kelly would have taken the train home Tuesday afternoon. Maybe the 2:40. Or the 8:00 evening.*
4. *The kidnappers knew exactly how much to ask for because Walton must have told them that was all that Inez could put together. Had they tortured him? Or was he a blabbermouth, an easy mark?*

Yeah, something was wrong. It was too pat. Too by-the-book. Detective Tracy began to theorize. Say Kelly Walton wanted to disappear into thin air. He had lost his job; he was fighting with his wife. So, what would he do to get his hands on the $10K he had saved? He would get himself "abducted" and have his accomplice pick up the money on 68th and Lexington. That's what he would do. Or he would pick it up himself - no, that would be too risky. Someone might see him and recognize him and his two-suit wardrobe. No, it was easier to have an accomplice. Some schmuck who would do his bidding. It had to be a man. But it was also possible Kelly Walton had a girlfriend on the side. Who knew?

Tracy picked up his coffee order and called the station. He had a couple of his assistants check the trains, the flights, and the bus routes for Kelly Walton's name. Maybe Mr. Kelly Walton wanted to disappear with the $10K, with no one the wiser, just like that. Next, Tracy went over his notes about the Walton's landlord and neighbors. There was something interesting about these folks. They were all a bit spooked. Was there reason to suspect that they were in on it? Maybe. But he hadn't detected any guilt. Just a cast of characters, like in a really bad out-of-town-and-never-making-it-to-Broadway play.

* * *

"I could disappear from the face of the earth,
and the world would go on."
- H. Murakami

Wednesday, 9:00 A.M. — Twelve hours earlier

Tracy woke up early and started with breakfast and a clean shave. He combed over the paper, nothing more than a quick glance. After feeding the menagerie of pets, he headed to his car. His first stop was going to be the apartment house where Kelly and Inez Walton lived.

The Regency Arms Apartments

The building was a bit run down on the exterior and could have been maintained a little bit better, but once you stepped inside the lobby, it was a different story. The walls, furniture, and ceiling were "art deco" in flavor, muted color palettes, and lots of bling. The lobby was stunning and yet warm at the same time. It reminded Tracy of a few of the old movie houses he had visited, like stepping back in time to another era where glitz and glamour reigned supreme.

He took the elevator up to the Walton apartment just to check on Inez and to see if she had heard any more from the kidnappers. Once inside the apartment, Tracy questioned the middle-aged woman. She said she had no communication from anyone; she seemed weary. He doubted she had slept much the night before. With a reassuring word, he left Inez and went back downstairs to the lobby. He had noticed the sign saying "building manager" on one of the doors beneath the stairs and to the left of the elevator. That was his first stop.

A man in a starched white shirt and dress pants answered on the first knock. He said his name was Bert Collins. But Tracy was thinking more along the line of Jack Lemon in suspenders. When Tracy showed his badge and told the man he had a few questions, Collins invited him into the office and indicated a low-back chair in the corner of the room. When both were settled in, Tracy began the interrogation. "I wonder if you could tell me, Mr. Collins. Are the Waltons good tenants?"

Bert Collins looked taken back, startled. "Wow, Detective. I wasn't expecting that. I thought maybe you were here about Mrs. Perez and her annoying little chihuahua. That dog barks night and day. At least until the pain in the ass and its owner went missing a few days ago. Don't know where Mrs. Perez is; no one does, not even her friends in the building. But she took the dog with her wherever she went. I say good riddance to her and the dog. But I don't wish any harm to come to them, of course. . .well, maybe the dog."

"No, sir, I don't know anything about Ms. Perez. I just want some information on Inez and Kelly Walton. Are they good tenants? Do they pay their rent on time? Are they. . .?"

"You can stop right there, Detective. Kelly and Inez are what landlords call "screamers." They argue a lot. I get complaints, especially from Mr. Drendall. He's their next-door neighbor. These old buildings, you know, they have thin walls. James Drendall can hear the dishes breaking from his living room. So can Mrs. Fletcher. I get complaints, Detective, but they are right on time with their rent. And I don't have any solid reason to evict them. I give them warnings, but they are mostly just scare tactics."

"Since you seem to know a lot about what goes on in your building, Mr. Collins, maybe you have noticed if Inez Walton has ever left with a suitcase. . . like maybe she was leaving Kelly or moving out."

"Yes, once. It was about six months ago. I don't think she got any further than the drugstore on the corner. She was flinging that suitcase around like it was pretty light, maybe even empty. It could have been a scare tactic of her own, not sure. But they patched up whatever it was because she was back in an hour, and it was pretty quiet for a few days. Then it started again."

"Does Mr. Walton ever get physical with his wife?"

"Naw. He's not the type. He's all talk. Loud talk but just talk."

"Okay, Mr. Collins. Thank you for the information."

Bert Collins' voice changed, dropped an octave or two. "Have the Waltons done something wrong, Detective Tracy? Something I should know about?"

"No, sir. Nothing. They have come to me for help with a little problem. And I just wanted to know if they were good people. Trustworthy. Now, I will need this Mr. Drendall's apartment number."

James Drendall and Mrs. Fletcher had both been checked out. They were very helpful. And, despite what the landlord said, neither had a bad thing to say about the Waltons, even with the fighting. Apparently, Inez and Kelly were likable and very neighborly. James Drendall had even been over to the Walton apartment for a few parties; and on occasion, a beer or two with Kelly during football games.

Tracy left the apartment building and stood on the sidewalk staring at the surrounding buildings. Inez had said that she felt as if she were being watched. Maybe from across the street. There were a lot of windows in that building; more than Tracy could cover in the amount of time he had before the ransom drop. He felt as if that was going to be his best bet at catching whoever was behind this abduction.

Unless, of course, Kelly Walton, with a little bit of help from a friend, had orchestrated his own disappearance to "take the money and run." John Payne would have done it that way. Ray Milland and James Mason, too. But was Kelly Walton really a film noir villain with a devious mind? Or just a schlep? Tracy had never met the man, so he couldn't be sure. All he knew was what Inez had told him from the very beginning, from their first meeting.

* * *

"He was disappearing a little more each day."
- A. Hoffman

Tuesday, 6 P.M. — 27 hours earlier

19th Precinct

Detective Nick Tracy was sitting at his desk thinking about the phone call from this Inez Walton woman. He should have been wrapping up reports on some of his other cases, but his mind kept going back to Inez and her phone call. He had promised that he would stop by and hear her story. Maybe even take a statement. He really wanted to help. He wasn't sure why. He was a homicide detective, but the case intrigued him. Tracy finished his work, grabbed his jacket, and headed out the precinct door.

The Apartment of Inez Walton

The apartment was nice, clean, everything in its place. . .and it smelled of cherries. Tracy took a seat on the chair in the front room and turned to the Walton woman with an inquiring look. Inez Walton was somewhere in her forties, with mousy brown hair and big eyes rimmed with cheap black make-up that made Tracy think of a raccoon he once saw on his uncle's porch. She had a voice that was a bit high and screechy, like an owl or fingernails on a blackboard. Tracy combed through his list of movie characters and could only come up with one similarity. Estelle Parsons. A very talented "B" actress who never really made it to the big time. But she had a great supporting role in *Bonnie and Clyde*, a classic from the sixties. Yeah, Estelle Parsons and her role as Blanche. . .that was Inez Walton, with eye shadow, liner, and a lot of pale lipstick.

"So, tell me, Ma'am, you received a call. Your instructions were to drop $10,000 in the trash can on the corner of 68th and Lexington at 4 o'clock tomorrow inside a newspaper. Do you have any idea why the ransom is for that specific amount? Is $10,000 significant in some way?"

Inez opened her eyes wide, just as Estelle would have done (method actress), and nodded her head. "Yes, Detective. It's the amount we have here in the apartment. In the safe. Kelly has never trusted banks much. We have been putting aside some each week, just until we got enough for a down payment on a place up north, a kind of getaway when the city becomes too overwhelming. We made a pact that when we got to $10,000, we would put the money in the bank and… don't ask, Detective. Kelly has a weird phobia. Putting the money in the bank would be my job, as Kelly is very superstitious. He won't set foot in a bank. So, I would be the one. But I don't mind. And then we could start looking for a sweet little house upstate."

"Do you think that your husband told the kidnappers you had that amount here in the apartment?"

"I do. I'm afraid they may have beat it out of him. Kelly guarded our little secret, he never told anyone about the money. . .but, if he feared for his life, don't you think he would tell them, Detective?"

"Yes, I do, Ms. Walton. And, of course, the kidnappers must know where you live, as they picked a trash can close to the apartment here."

Tracy took a deep breath. "…Can you tell me, Ms. Walton, do you know anyone who would be so bold as to do this to you and your husband? And, by the way, what does Mr. Walton do for a living?"

"He works uptown as a salesman for a big import/export company. Remco Imports. They handle many products from overseas. But Kelly and his boss don't get along. Mr. Fischer had a huge Christmas party last year, everyone in the sales department got invited. . .except Kelly. Fischer said the invite must have gotten lost in the mail, but we knew better. It was a deliberate snub."

"So, other than this boss, Mr. Fischer, is there anyone who has a grudge against your husband? How about on the personal side? Any ex-wives? Or bitter friends?"

"No, Detective. And certainly no one powerful enough to pull off his abduction in broad daylight. That would take a lot of planning, don't you think? Someone who knew he would be coming home from the job interview in Boston. By train."

"Yes, it would. Also, he would've had to be willing to go with someone. Perhaps someone he knew, which is why I asked about his recent activities. And, of course, he has to be held somewhere. Here in the city is my guess. These guys are taking a chance holding him for twenty-four hours. Someone has to stay in the room to guard him."

Tracy had a vision of a large import/export

warehouse. Lots of room to hide someone. And someone who knew he had an appointment in Boston. Maybe someone in this company Remco Imports. "Okay, Mrs. Walton, I think I have enough to get me started. Try not to worry. I know that's easy for me to say, but most kidnappers don't harm their victims. The victim is their golden goose. They need them to complete the transaction. I will get back with you first thing in the morning, early, so try and get some sleep if you can."

Tracy left the Walton apartment and headed home. The apartment was dark and cold when he arrived. The "menagerie" greeted him with wagging tails and a few friendly barks. When he was seated at his dining room table, and everyone had been fed their evening meal, Tracy opened a can of soup and then called the train station and checked on the train times. When he had a complete schedule in front of him, he studied it carefully. He wasn't sure why, but the times seemed to be important. Maybe a key to how the kidnappers got Kelly Walton off the train and into their grasp. He had to have been picked up at Penn Station.

Tracy made a note or two in his book and then went to the couch to stretch out. Bogart jumped up to join him. It was late. He had stayed a bit too long at the Walton apartment. He was tired. Weary. He was remembering that first call to the station by Inez Walton, when his head hit the pillow.

* * *

"We are lost because we chose to disappear."
- S. Wilson

Tuesday, 5 P.M. — 28 hours earlier

The 19th Precinct

Detective Tracy was having a busy day. In fact,

everyone was busy. Especially the Special Unit squad. So that was how Tracy became the recipient of a call that came into the station late in the day on a Tuesday afternoon. It was a call about a kidnapping. Or, in this case, a husband nabbing.

Some woman on the Upper West Side wanted to speak to someone in the station about her husband being held for ransom. And Tracy took the call. Not that he wanted to, but he was feeling generous that day. His life was in order, and he felt charitable. And the switchboard said she sounded scared. The woman's name was Inez Walton, and her husband of eight years, Kelly H. Walton, was being held for a ransom that she needed to pay by four o'clock the next day. The drop was on the Upper East Side, a trash can. It sounded a little fishy to Tracy, but he promised to follow up. Maybe he would stop in to see Ms. Walton on his way home. She didn't live far from his apartment. Kidnapping was not in his realm of homicide, but the poor woman sounded upset, desperate for help.

"Give me your apartment number, Ms. Walton, and I will stop by in a few hours and take a statement."

"Oh no, Detective. What if the kidnappers are watching? They told me not to call the police."

"It's highly unlikely, Ms. Walton, that they would be hanging around, taking a chance of being spotted and ID'd later. But I am a plain clothes detective. They won't know I'm a cop. How many apartments are in your building?"

"Twelve," the frightened woman answered.

"Well then, I could be visiting any number of those apartments. Not necessarily yours. Pull the street side shades on your window if it makes you feel better. And believe me, I will make sure I am not followed into your building. I have ways."

"Okay, Detective, if you are sure…" The woman's voice trailed off, and she hung up abruptly; no good-bye,

no thank you. When the line was clear, Tracy ran a check
on Kelly and Inez Walton from the Upper East Side. There
were no outstanding warrants. There were no priors. There
was nothing. The Waltons were clean as a whistle. Law-
abiding citizens who just wanted to live in peace? That was
the read that Tracy got. Was he right? Only time would tell.

* * *

*"Disappear along with the sunset, never to rise
again."*
- M. Khan

Tuesday, 4:00 P.M. — 29 hours earlier

***The Regency Arms Apartments, Upper East Side
Manhattan***

Inez Walton was smiling. Big. Her husband Kelly
would be home in a few hours from Boston, and he would
be excited to see his favorite pie cooling on the pie rack.
Inez was a pleaser. . .and she made great pies, especially
cherry ones, which were Kelly's favorite. Mr. Hernandez at
the fruit stand always saved a basket of his best cherries for
Inez. Only fresh ones would do. Kelly could tell the fresh
ones from the day-olds every time.

Inez smiled again. Tonight just might be special.
Kelly had gone to Boston on a job interview. A good one.
Not that his job at Remo Corporation wasn't a good one.
No. But Kelly was always trying to better himself. That's
what had first attracted Inez to him. That "get up and go"
attitude. He was never still. Her strong Puerto Rican family
had not liked Kelly at first, only because he was considered
a *blanquito*, a white boy. But they had come around
eventually, especially after Kelly had started shelling out
money whenever her brothers hit rough spots or her parents
wanted to vacation in the motherland.

57

Inez sighed. Life was good, and she was content. Well, as content as she could be for a woman who wished she could be born again, only two sizes smaller. At least she knew her pies were going to be a treat. She just needed to concentrate on finishing before Kelly walked through that door. In fact, Inez Walton was so intent on her pie-making that she almost didn't hear the phone ring. By the fourth ring, it occurred to her that there was a loud noise coming from the living room, almost drowning out her favorite soap opera playing on the small kitchen television. (*Oh, if only Carolyn would leave Bradley and move on with her life, be with Phillip.*)

"Hello. . .yes, this is Inez Walton," the housewife said into the mouthpiece in her sexiest voice, the one she always used for phone calls; it made her feel good, maybe a little bit younger, prettier. But what the caller had to say was not so nice. Inez dropped the dish towel in her hand and stared at the telephone as if it had turned into a viper about to latch onto her arm.

"Wait. What is this? How do I know that you…I don't know if that's enough time…Yes, but…No, I won't say anything to anyone and I…" The line had suddenly gone dead.

Inez threw the phone and ran to the bathroom. After throwing up most of what she had eaten earlier, she washed her face, combed her hair, and sat down hard on the bathroom floor. How did they know about the $10,000? She and Kelly weren't wealthy. They were comfortable. They had everything they wanted except kids. They had tried, but Kelly wasn't able. And how did they know she had that amount of cash in the house? They, whoever *they* were, must have beaten it out of Kelly. Poor thing. He could be lying in a ditch somewhere. What a terrible thought. Or tied up and gagged. He could be knocked out. He could be…No, no. She wouldn't think the worst. That was too horrible to even consider.

Inez pulled herself up from the bathroom floor, ran to the desk, and wrote down the instructions she had been given. If only she would have done the same with the name of the hotel where Kelly said he was staying in Boston. She was so scatter-brained; she couldn't remember anything. *The Bostonian?? The Embassy?? The ????? Oh, why didn't she write it down?*

Next, Inez went to the small wall safe and took out the money. She stared at the stack of $100 bills. And then she whirled around and looked out the den window to the building across the street. Was there someone watching her from one of those windows? Did they have binoculars trained on her right now? Or while she had gone about making her pies? Oh, wait - there was a flash of light, like a reflection off a lens. A binocular lens? Yes, that was it. Someone was watching her. Maybe to make sure she showed up tomorrow. Maybe, if she didn't, they would come into the apartment after her. Maybe hurt her, threaten her, or, God forbid, *kill* her.

Inez grabbed her head and pressed on her temples. Over and over. How could this have happened? Someone must have grabbed Kelly and made him talk. And they had held him for ransom somewhere. Yes, that had to be it. Was he in some shady part of town? Maybe he was hurt. Maybe he was in some dark and cold place. With that image of Kelly, his hands tied, his feet bound, and his mouth duct-taped closed, Inez Walton started to cry. She couldn't help it. She knew that night she would sleep with the $10,000 under the covers with her, lying beside her. She had to make sure nothing happened to the money before tomorrow at 4 o'clock. And, even though they told her not to, maybe she should call the police. Maybe she was going to need help.

Inez sat down on the couch, clutching the money to her chest, and closed her eyes and prayed. When she finished, she made the sign of the cross on her chest and

reached for the princess phone. She dialed "0" for the
operator. The next twenty-eight hours would begin with,
"Give me the police."

* * *

*"The only comfort I had was in the planning to
disappear." - A. Mathis*

Tuesday, 7 A.M. - 3 P.M. — 30 hours earlier

***An Apartment on the East Side, The Office of the Western
Union Telegraph Company***

Nothing ever happened in Stanley K. Smith's life,
which was as boring as his name. He had often asked his
mother why she couldn't have given him a nice exotic first
name, just to counterbalance the Smith part, which was so
mundane vanilla he couldn't stand it. Something like
Xavier or Antonio or even something biblical like Moses or
Barnabus. But she had only laughed and told him he should
be thankful he was alive and healthy. And then she would
leave the room as if he was boring her as well.

So it wasn't surprising that Stanley K. Smith woke
up one day and decided to change his life. That day. He
was going to do something he had never done before.
Maybe he would take a different route to work. Or go
somewhere different for lunch. Maybe at lunch he would
have tuna on toast instead of his usual turkey on rye.
Maybe he would call an old girlfriend, one of only two he
had ever had in his life. Or maybe he would just forget the
whole thing and take his mother's advice and be thankful
he had any sort of life at all. He told himself to "look at the
Kennedy brothers." It still pained him to stare into the face
of Bobby Kennedy in the photo on his wall above his desk
where the candidate for President was on the campaign trail

shaking hands from the back of a truck bed. A few months later, he would be gunned down. Dead, no life. He had been the same age as Stanley was now. Forty-two.

With a sigh, Stanley K. Smith finished his boring breakfast of Melba toast and oatmeal and dressed for work. He did decide on a different tie at the last minute. Maybe that was his break from the mundane. But no, no. . . it had to be something bigger, much bigger. Something he would remember for a long time and maybe look back and say, "That was the moment that I changed my life." But Stanley K. Smith knew it would never happen. Sometimes you think you want to do something and then just disappear. But what you really want is to be found.

Stanley arrived at the Western Union office on time, 9 o'clock sharp, even though he had been bold enough to take a different route. Thankfully, it hadn't cost him more than a minute or two. Sitting down at his desk, where he took up too much space, Stanley greeted his co-workers and nodded to his boss. That's the only greeting Stanley ever gave Mr. Roberts: just a nod, nothing more. He then went about his day, which consisted of mostly humdrum work. No skills required, as Stanley K. Smith had none.

Around two o'clock, almost at the end of his shift, he received an order over his teleprinter on the ½ inch-wide gummed tape. He slipped on his thimble cutter and then transferred the gum tape to one of the forms in his bin. He typed out the usual preamble showing the number of the sender, the time sent, the handling post office, and the number of words. The second line showed the name and address of the recipient, which was followed by the tape from the sender. At the bottom of the form, he typed in a few distinguishing repeated words so everything could be double-checked.

When he was done, Stanley K. Smith stared at the message. It was what Western Union called an AP 8. Someone had paid a little extra money for expediency. An overnight would have been half the price, but, hey, what did Stanley care? He was just an employee of Western Union. Or wait, was that all he really was? Stanley Smith picked up a New York City phone book and checked for a listing. And there it was in black and white. The address matched. It wasn't far away from where he now sat, contemplating something he had never done before. Maybe this was it. Maybe this was a sign. He wrote the phone number on a piece of paper and stuffed it in his pocket.

Then the meek little no-life man made an excuse to leave; he said he was sick and coming down with something bad and contagious. Then he walked through the front door of the Western Union Telegraph office, whistling. He stopped at the pay phone just down the street and dialed the number he had found in the phone book that the city of New York so kindly provided. And, when the woman on the other end answered, Stanley just blurted out whatever came into his slightly warped mind. He had used words like: *kidnapped. . .your husband. . .$10,000. . .trash can on Lexington and 68th. . .don't call the police.* And then he slammed down the phone booth phone. Just like that. What did he have to lose? If it worked, it worked. If it didn't, then so be it. All he had to do was wait twenty-four hours, and then he would collect the money from that trash can. Maybe he would pay someone else to do it. But who? Stanley K. Smith didn't have any friends. But no worries. He would figure something out when the time came.

And just like that, Stanley K. Smith changed his life. Sometimes you think you want to disappear, but what you really want is to be found. Right!? But Stanley wasn't disappearing. Telegrams were. They were a dying form of communication. Not many were sent nowadays. In another few years, the way Stanley K. Smith figured it, they would probably be obsolete, gone. Like milkmen, ice delivery trucks, and horse drawn carriages. Poof. No more words on a flimsy piece of paper. With a smile on his face, Stanley stepped out of the phone booth, retrieved the number he had written from his pocket, and tore up the undelivered telegram he was clutching in his hot little hands. The one that was addressed to Inez Walton on the Upper East Side that said:

Plans changed **stop** *Staying an extra night in Boston to celebrate* **stop** *Tried to call you no answer* **stop** *Be home tomorrow Wednesday on the 8 pm train* **stop** *Take the ten thousand $ out of safe and put in bank* **stop** *Have good news, love Kelly*

THE CHRISTMAS IN MARCH MURDER

PROLOGUE

> " 'Twas the night before Christmas,
> when all through the house... "
> - C.C. Moore

Ryland Reese was a fanatic. *But was that really such a bad thing?* Ryland felt the word had gotten a bad rap over the years. First off, Ryland was a fanatic about the letter "R". When he married some thirty years ago, he had decided that his children would all be given names beginning with "R", thus ensuring that his heirs would have double "R" names, like himself. Some say he had even married his lovely wife Rhonda for this very reason. But Ryland would remark that was silly. "Just look at her," he would say, "who wouldn't want to marry her?' Thankfully, their marriage had been a long and loving one.

Ryland Reese was also a fanatic about many other things as well: the New York Giants, Oldsmobile cars, citrus fruits, the Andy Griffith Show reruns, the tie counter at Macy's, the Beatles, and family game night. But the one thing that the middle-aged Ryland Reese was most fanatical about was Christmas. He loved Christmas. Christmas was his passion; it was his life - at least *most* of his life, since Rhonda had died a few years earlier, leaving him alone with a lot of time on his hands and three grown children who were busy with their own lives. And, even though Ryland Reese honored and revered the Holy part of Christmas, the birth of Jesus Christ of Nazareth, and knew his bible backward and forward while attending his local church faithfully every Sunday, Ryland's favorite part of Christmas was the side that perpetuated the notion that a jolly old man with a long white beard, a red suit and a twinkle in his eye came down the chimney every year and put presents for good little girls and boys under a decorated tree in your living room. So, Ryland Reese of Staten Island, New York started preparing for Christmas in the spring. He took January and February off to catch up on his life. But come March, Ryland began making any needed repairs to his Christmas decorations: changing burned-out bulbs on his strings of Christmas lights, cleaning garland, replacing any broken ornaments, changing the red plaid ribbons on his plastic wreaths, freshening Santa's costume, checking on the mechanical workings of every one of his elves, and covering all manner of repairs to his beloved decorations. It took months of planning to get everything just right.

Ryland Reese's neighbors barely bothered to decorate their own houses, as no one on the block could compete with Ryland. He was the king of this middle-class neighborhood in the fifth borough of New York, when it came to all things Christmas. He started putting up his displays the first of October and always finished by Halloween when all the little kiddies in the neighborhood came trick-or-treating. Due to lack of time and energy, Ryland didn't decorate for Easter or 4th of July (even though he was as patriotic as they came). Only Christmas. The mother of all holidays. And this year was going to be something special. Ryland had come up with an idea for a sled and eight reindeer who were going to be strung across his roof while a life-size Santa would be seen halfway down the chimney. That meant, of course, that he would not be able to use his fireplace until January, but Ryland Reese would be content with central heat.

So, on March 4th Ryland began the process. He had Santa, his reindeer, his sled, and all of the Christmas lights stretched out on the lawn in his backyard. Ryland had only to make one last trip up to the roof to make sure his measurements were correct. These yearly trips to the roof were necessary in Ryland's mind, even though he was getting on in years and had added an extra ten pounds to his waistline. The way Ryland saw it, at fifty-three, he was still a young man who was fit enough to make the climb up that ladder. Some time ago, he had rigged a nice little safety rope just to be sure nothing went wrong, or God forbid that he should slip and fall. And this year it was all going to be perfect.

Ryland attached the safety rope around his waist and made the climb up the old wood ladder. When he was done with his measuring, he started his descent. And that's when Ryland Reese lost his footing. His last thoughts may have been, "No problem, the safety rope will hold me." But the truth was, it wouldn't. Ryland Reese, age 53, the Railroad Street Christmas fanatic of Staten Island, New York, fell to his death off his shingled roof. Just like that.

* * *

"...Not a creature was stirring, not even a mouse..." - C.C. Moore

Detective Nick Tracy of the Manhattan 19th Precinct called the boys at the Staten Island Precinct when he heard about the death of Ryland Reese, just to make sure there had not been any evidence of foul play. And there was not.

A simple case of an accidental death. The man had gone up his ladder and then fallen from his roof and broken his neck. He had died instantly.

Tracy had known Ryland Reese for quite some time, ever since the man who loved Christmas had helped solve a homicide aboard the Staten Island Ferry almost twenty years back. Tracy had been part of the case in a minor way; he was still in his rookie year. Through the months of investigation, the young detective and the very observant witness became friends. The ten-year difference in their age had never been a problem. Tracy always came by the Reese house after Thanksgiving to check out Ryland's Christmas display and usually ended up staying for a few beers. Especially since Rhonda had passed away unexpectedly. Tracy had gone to the funeral and then spent the afternoon getting drunk with Ryland after all the mourners had extended their condolences and returned to their own homes and their own lives.

But Nick Tracy and Ryland Reese have lost touch recently. And Tracy needed to know more. So, after speaking with the responding officer at the Staten Island Precinct, Tracy made a call to Ryland's daughter, Rachel. And Rachel Reese had been very specific.

"Something is wrong, Nick. I know it. Dad told me a few things. I think you need to check into his death. I don't believe for one minute that it was an accident."

Tracy was shocked. The air in his chest deflated.

"What makes you say that, Rachel?"

"It's a bunch of stuff. He told me he wasn't sleeping well. He had been getting threatening letters."

"What kind of threats?"

"Like telling him not to put up his Christmas decorations. That if he did, they would be destroyed. And you know that would have devastated him. Since Mom died, Christmas decorating is all that he lives for. Other than my brothers and I."

"Did he have any idea who was sending the letters? Or. . .?"

"I'm sorry, Nick. I can't talk. I'm late, and everyone is waiting for me to make funeral arrangements. Could we meet at the house soon? Maybe tomorrow? I have something for you."

Of course, he could. Rachel had managed to plant a seed of doubt in Nick Tracy's mind. Despite what the officers in the investigating precinct said, it sounded like there was more to this case than just an accidental fall off a roof.

They always say, "This is how it starts." Just a shadow of a doubt. An inkling of suspicion, skepticism, uncertainty. And then it builds. . .*Who would want to murder the man who loved Christmas?*

* * *

"...The stockings were hung..."
- C.C. Moore

Detective Tracy and Rachel Reese were sitting side by side at the kitchen table in the house where her father had lived for twenty-nine years, which at this moment seemed a bit more dated and disheveled than Tracy remembered. Rachel was in her early twenties with a face like her father's, blonde hair, and green eyes that were now red and swollen. Tracy doubted she had slept more than a few hours.

"Okay, Rachel. Tell me what your father said. Everything."

"He said someone was threatening him. They were sending him notes through the mail. Somebody didn't want him to display his Christmas decorations. And they said they would destroy his lovely collection if he dared to put them up."

"But why?"

"I don't know Nick. Do you think it's someone in the neighborhood? Sure, there are a lot of cars driving by to see the display; sometimes the street does get a bit clogged, but this seems so extreme. These neighbors are some of his best friends. They have parties together. They have raised their kids together. I grew up in this house, and I can't think of anyone who would want to hurt Dad."

"What about in the family? Was your dad on good terms with your brothers and their wives?"

"Yes. You know Ronnie can get a little hot-headed. And Remmie is always borrowing money for one scheme or another. But my brothers loved Dad. They wouldn't hurt him."

"What about friends? Or business acquaintances? Are there any that you might suspect?"

"No."

"But you still think there's more to the 'falling off the roof' story?"

Rachel Reese stood and left the room for a moment. When she returned, she was carrying a rope. She handed it to Tracy. "The police didn't say anything. But you can see the end of that safety rope has been cut."

Tracy turned the rope over and over in his hand. The end did seem to have a clean slice. Why hadn't the Staten Island station caught this? Did they just accept the "accident" theory because it happened so often? Because everyone knows someone who has fallen off a roof at one time or another? "Do you have anything else that leads you to believe that your dad may have been killed?"

Once again, Rachel left the room. When she returned, she was clutching an envelope. On the outside, in decidedly male handwriting, were the words:
NICK TRACY, MERRY CHRISTMAS.

Tracy glanced at Rachel Reese and then back to the envelope, which he tore open with the tip of his finger. Inside was a note. Just a few lines from an old children's

poem, *'Twas the Night Before Christmas,* written by C.C.
Moore, years before.....*Away to the window I flew like a
flash. Tore open the shutters and threw up the sash. . .More
rapid than eagles his courses they came and he whistled
and shouted and called them by name.* Then Ryland Reese
had listed the names of Santa's reindeer. Followed by
further lines from the poem. . .*from the top of the porch, to
the top of the wall. Now dash away! Dash away! Dash
away all!*

Tracy looked up from the paper, his eyes met
Rachel's. "What the hell does this mean?"

Rachel shook her head. "I don't know. He told me if
anything happened to him to give the envelope to you. That
you were the best detective in the world. I promised him I
would. He made me swear. I should have called you the
minute I got the news of his fall. He was worried, Nick. But
you know Dad. He would blow things off. But I think this
time was different. What this old kid's poem has to do with
anything I don't know."

"I wish I did, Rachel. But I have no idea what he's
trying to tell me. Why didn't you call me when all of this
started? Maybe I could have helped. And it looks to me as
if someone sabotaged this safety line. For some reason,
someone didn't want your dad to put up those decorations.
But why kill him?"

"What about this part: *From the top of the porch to
the top of the wall?* Wait now…"

As if suddenly hit with an idea, Rachel stood and
worked her way through the house and exited the back
door. Tracy trailed after her. The two spent thirty minutes
looking everywhere on the old porch. They even took the
swing apart and pried open a few of the loose baseboards.
Nothing. Exhausted and covered with dust and debris, the
two re-entered the house and went straight to the kitchen to
clean up.

"I am going to start an investigation, Rachel. I don't

want you to do anything. Meet me here in 48 hours with your brothers and their wives. I hope to have something for you by then."

Rachel nodded as she dried her hands on the old dishcloth. "Okay. I will. I just hope that we aren't in for any more surprises."

That, of course, was an understatement.

* * *

". . .While visions of sugar plums . . ."
- C.C. Moore

Tracy decided to start his investigation by calling on the neighbors. His first stop was Bill and Thelma White, who lived next door to the Reese house. Bill had deep furrows in his brow as if worrying were a daily event for the middle-aged man. From what he told Tracy, the previous years of recession had taken him totally hostage. He had been out of a job for quite some time and had sought refuge inside his home. Tracy waited for the man whose tee-shirt was decorated with mustard stains to add more details to his story, but he stopped talking abruptly. And even though both Bill and Thelma White were quite concerned about the death of their neighbor, they could offer little in the way of information. They didn't see or hear anything that night. But Thelma did say she thought she saw Remmie Reese's car. But she also implied that she could be mistaken. Tracy placed his card on the foyer table as he left.

The next stop on the neighborhood canvas was on the other side of Ryland Reese's house. The home of Punky and Sonja Lutz. When Tracy knocked on the door, he didn't know what to expect. Certainly not a grown man the size of a mountain who went by the name of Punky. But there he was. Sonja wasn't home, so Tracy spent the next thirty minutes with Punky, who was trying to be helpful but didn't have much to add. He heard that Ryland had fallen off the roof, but Punky said he wasn't surprised.

"He went up there on that roof too much. It was bound to happen someday. I told him to let his son do all that placement stuff, but he didn't pay me no heed."

(Tracy was trying to listen, but it was hard to take anything seriously coming from a man who continued to call himself Punky after the age of ten.)

The next stop was the house directly across the street from the Reese house. A single man by the name of Frank Mendola, who was short and stocky, with thinning hair and a prematurely wrinkled face. After they had been seated at the kitchen table and Tracy had an iced tea in front of him at the insistence of Mr. Mendola, the man informed him that he had been the one to find Ryland lying on the ground at the foot of the ladder.

"It was awful, Detective. I knew he was gone, but I called the Staten Island police, and they called an ambulance. It was tough. I had a soft spot for Ryland. We moved into our houses on the very same day. We both had wives back then."

Tracy listened to a few old "war stories" from Frank Mendola and then thanked him for the information on the way out the door, which Tracy noticed faced directly across from that of Ryland Reese's.

The next two stops were at the homes of a pair of spinsters. A Ginny Adison and a Carrie Rhodes. Both women were cordial, but they didn't have much to add to the investigation. They spent more time trying to get Tracy to sample their cooking than actually talking about Ryland Reese. Tracy obliged a few taste tests, but he felt a bit uncomfortable after Carrie Rhodes made a few suggestive remarks. Tracy was careful not to let his green eyes stray to her hazel ones as he made his notes, thanked the women, and then moved on.

Next, he knocked on the door of a nice little white

house with green awnings. The mailbox had the name Tillman written in big black letters. The man who answered Tracy's knock directed Tracy to the dining room, where he indicated a seat and then pulled up a chair backwards for himself. His eyes were large, almost too big for his stone-faced head and his body too big for his shirt. The buttonholes were stretched sideways. Tillman kept his words short and neat.

"No, I didn't see the accident, Detective. But I heard the ambulance when it turned on the street. Ryland was going to fall off that roof one day. He was getting too old. I offered to go up there for him, but he wouldn't hear of it."

After asking Mr. Tillman if he knew of anyone who was upset about the Christmas decorations, Tracy took his leave from the Tillman house. He had the sense that Bick Tillman suspected something was very wrong. He was the first of the neighbors to inquire as to why a detective was asking questions about an accidental fall off a roof.

The last stop on the street was a nice house with landscaping fit for an English country estate; so finely laid out that Tracy suspected the owner must spend a great deal of time on his yard or had a gardener that had won a few awards. The man who answered the door said his name was James Scranton, but insisted, "Please call me Jimmie, Detective." And so, he did. Jimmie was young, recently divorced (apparently, the marriage had collapsed during the honeymoon when the stars had disappeared from the new Mrs. Scranton's eyes) and he was well-off. Jimmie tried to be helpful, he had really liked Ryland, but he could offer very little. Tracy left the man as soon as possible.

Once out on the sidewalk, Tracy checked a few things in his notebook and made an entry. There was one thing that everyone had agreed upon. When asked, "Were there any cars parked on the street that night other than the neighbors?" all of those he had interrogated answered the same way: "I think I saw Remmie Reese's car somewhere…"

Night was falling by the time Tracy finished the rounds. Through a break in the clouds, he could see a sprinkling of bright stars that formed a carpet of light in the darkened sky. Later, Tracy would have a hard time remembering why he hadn't explored further and asked more questions. Ryland Reese had once told him that men who start wars never attend them. They give orders with a pen and paper and call themselves leaders. But they are not leading; they are watching. Tracy decided he wanted to be much more than "a watcher."

* * *

"…When out on the lawn…"
- C.C. Moore

Just as they'd planned it, Tracy met up with Rachel, Remmie, and Ronnie Reese at their father's house the next morning. After the condolences were out of the way, Tracy got straight to the point. "I'm so sorry for your loss, kids, but I'm here to help. From what you have told me, someone was threatening your father, sending him notes telling him not to put up his Christmas decorations and that if he did, they would destroy them and keep destroying them."

Tracy looked to Remmie first. He was a tall man in his early twenties, not much older than Rachel. He, too, had light hair and eyes, but he was thinner than his siblings. Almost gaunt, compared to Ronnie, who was just turning twenty-two and was more robust. "Remmie, do you have any idea who might want to harm your father? Perhaps even kill him?"

"No, Nick. I don't."

Tracy took out the note. He laid it on the table in front of both boys. "Your Dad left me this note. It's just a couple of lines from an old Christmas poem. Does it mean anything to either one of you?"

Both boys read the note over carefully. Ronnie offered a suggestion. "Rachel told us about the note. She said that you looked on the porch and the wall. But what about this other line. . .*Tore open the shutters and threw up the sash?*"

Tracy turned to Rachel. "We didn't think of that. Where are the shutters? In Ryland's office?"

All four people stood at the same time and headed down the hallway in complete silence. They entered Ryland Reese's den. It was dark and musty, as if it had been closed up for some time. The four went straight to the first window inside the doorway. Rachel reached up and opened the wooden shutter. Nothing. They then moved to the next pair of shutters with the same results. The last pair of shutters were behind Ryland's desk; they were difficult to reach, but Rachel managed. When she pulled open the slats, a VHS tape fell out. It must have been lodged in between the window and the wood frame. Ronnie picked up the tape lying at his feet and crossed the room to the tape player sitting atop the television. He popped in the tape and hit play.

The image that appeared was of a Christmas party. There were twenty or so people milling around the Reese living room. Rachel, Ronnie, and Remmie were visible. Tracy also recognized all of the neighbors that he had called upon the previous day. The rest were unidentified.

"Who are all these other people?" Tracy asked.

"Friends, a couple of relatives, mostly neighbors," Remmie replied.

Before Tracy could ask any further questions, the tape came to an end. Remmie shook his head. "That tape couldn't be any more than three minutes long. I remember that Christmas party. It was the year before last when Dad was trying out his new camera. I remember watching the tape the next day. It was longer than that. So why is there only three minutes?"

"Your dad wanted me to see something on that tape. I think I need to speak with everyone at the party that night. I've already interviewed the Whites and the Lutzes and a few others on the block."

Rachel interrupted. "You can meet everyone at the funeral this afternoon. They have all indicated that they are attending. The relatives, of course, will be there."

Tracy pushed the eject button and slipped the tape into his pocket along with the note from Ryland Reese.

"It is obvious that your father is trying to tell me something. I need to find out what. And Remmie, were you here at the house the night your dad fell? There are a few neighbors who would swear they saw your car parked on the street outside the house."

Remmie Reese looked shocked. And then angry."No, I was not here. And my car certainly wasn't parked anywhere nearby. They were mistaken. A white car looks like every other white car in the world from a distance."

Tracy made a mental note and then started back for the door. "I will see you all at the funeral. Just make sure I get to meet all of the people who appear on the tape."

* * *

". . .The moon on the breast. . ."
- C.C. Moore

Fitzpatrick's Funeral home was crowded. There were enough chairs for everyone in attendance at Ryland Reese's service: family, neighbors, friends, and one police detective. Nick Tracy sat at the back of the row of folding chairs and observed. Funny how people react to death. Everyone has a different reaction. Some attendees went right up to the mahogany casket to pay their respects quietly. Some cried. Others just stared. Tracy spotted the Reese family: the two boys and their wives and Rachel. They nodded in Tracy's direction but waited until the service was over to offer any introductions.

The first of those introductions was Jeff Connors, the nephew of Ryland Reese, a young man with a million-dollar smile who had champagne taste and cheap beer money, according to Ronnie and Remmie, who had given Tracy a pre-intro-run-down. Tracy immediately became suspicious of the nephew, who, even though he had good looks and an extensive vocabulary, was a bit of a pompous jerk. Maybe the nephew needed money, and Ryland was reluctant to loan him anymore. Maybe the nephew made threats to try and test the blackmail waters. Wouldn't be the first time. Tracy had seen the extortion method used many times over the years. But a quick question regarding his whereabouts on the night of the murder turned suspicion into mush. Jeff Connors, the son of Ryland's sister, was out of town that night, apparently on a job, according to the man himself and verified by his mother who had joined the conversation. Tracy offered his condolences to both and then left the circle.

His next stop in the room full of mourners were a few of the neighbors he had met the previous day. He didn't waste much time, as he already had their statements. Rachel rescued him from Punky Lutz and made an introduction to a woman on the tape who was a neighbor at the end of the street. Beatrice Emory. She was a large, rotund woman with an attractive face and eyes that sparkled in the light coming through the funeral home windows. After a few minutes with Beatrice, Tracy moved on without a single bit of new information.

Crossing the room with determined steps, Tracy made his way to the enormous foyer and sat for a moment making some notes. Suddenly he felt a presence breathing over his shoulder. When he turned, he was face to face with

Remmie Reese.

"Sorry, Nick. I didn't mean to startle you. I wasn't reading over your shoulder or anything. I was just wondering if you had formed any impressions. . . of this group."

"Nothing new. I think I've met everyone on the tape. At least everyone we can see. There were a few people in the shadows, but none of their faces were visible so I don't think Ryland was trying to tell me anything about them."

"I agree." Remmie Reese nodded but then turned back at the last minute. "You know Nick, there's someone who wasn't on the tape. She was standing with Dad while he was filming. Her name is Jennifer Bates. She had a thing for Dad. Hard to believe, I mean he wasn't exactly Paul Newman. But she always seemed to be in the picture."

"Except in this case?"

"Remmie chuckled. "Yeah. And even though she was standing beside him, I thought maybe you might want to talk to her."

"Okay, kid. Point her out."

Remmie walked out of the foyer with Tracy close on his heels. When they were back in the funeral home's main room Remmie nodded in the direction of an attractive woman a few rows ahead of where they were standing and then left while Tracy turned his attention to Jennifer Bates. The woman looked distraught. She was sitting in one of the chairs provided by the funeral parlor, but her body was almost rigid as if she wanted as little contact as possible with the vinyl-covered chair. Someone sat down beside her and she turned her head to speak, but the rest of her body remained behind. Tracy could now see that she was grieving. He made the instant decision not to intrude on Jennifer Bates' privacy. On the way out the front door, he made a few more notes.

Was it possible that Remmie Reese was guilty?

Who stands to inherit money from Ryland's death? The children. And who needed money the most? Remmie. Tracy recalled a statement by Ryland's oldest son: "Dad spent thousands on Christmas ornaments each year, replacing this and replacing that, but he gave us the cheesiest gifts. He wouldn't spend a dime on his own children."

Was Remmie harboring resentment? More than likely. The question: Had Remmie crossed the line? Or had the time for crossing the line been many lines ago? The evidence was sketchy.

Tracy got into his car and left the funeral home with little more than he had arrived with.

* * *

"...When what to my wondering eyes..."
- C.C. Moore

The funeral had been interesting but not exactly eye-opening. Tracy had learned a bit about the family. After ruling out Ronnie as a suspect, Tracy still couldn't take Remmie off the list. Ryland's son knew he stood to inherit a great deal of Ryland Reese's estate. A nice little windfall would certainly solve his problems. And then there was the fact that all the neighbors seemed to believe that Remmie's car was parked on the street that night. It seemed odd that they all thought the same thing. But if it was Remmie, why go to the bother of sending threatening letters about the decorations? Why not just plan to cut the rope? Everyone knew that Ryland spent a great deal of time in the spring on the roof planning the layout for the decorations. Anyone could have cut that rope. Or had someone do it for them.

Tracy arrived home, kicked off his shoes, and changed out of his dress clothes. After feeding the animals and playing a game of tug-of-war with Bogart and Winston, he slipped into a pair of sweatpants and a t-shirt, poured a beer, and went to sit on his old, worn leather chair that used to be light tan. All the dogs followed his move. Next, he popped the Ryland Reese videotape into his player and watched a few times. Then, he made a list of each person on the tape that the kids had identified.

- *Remmie Reese (son) - playing Santa Claus*
- *Rachel Reese (daughter) - playing Mrs. Claus*
- *Ronnie Reese (son) - elf hat giving out presents*
- *Jeff Connors (nephew) - elf hat carrying trash bags*
- *Bill White (next-door neighbor) - pouring beers from the keg*
- *Thelma White (wife of Bill) - laying out food*
- *Punky Lutz (next door neighbor) - at record player picking out music*
- *Sonja Lutz (wife of Punky) - turning on tree lights and adjusting ornaments*
- *Frank Mendola (neighbor) - singing along with the music*
- *Ginny Adison (neighbor) - pouring punch*
- *Bick Tillman (neighbor) - dancing to music*
- *Carrie Rhodes (neighbor) - giving out silverware*
- *Jimmie Scranton (neighbor) - sitting on couch doing nothing*

A bunch of mundane and typical Christmas party activities. Nobody looked like they were doing anything unusual or suspect. So, what was Ryland Reese trying to tell him? It had to be something so discreet that anyone finding the note or the tape had no idea what Ryland Reese was trying to tell a detective with the New York City police department.

Tracy slipped on his tennis shoes, piled the dogs in his car, and left the house. The drive to Staten Island over the Verrazzano Bridge went quickly this time of night without heavy traffic. When Tracy arrived at the Reese house, he left the dogs in the car. They followed every step of his departure, watching out of the car windows while he went to find the old ladder. It was leaning up alongside the shed in the backyard. Tracy placed it against the house and made the climb that Ryland Reese had made for years. Once on the roof, Tracy stared into the backyards of every neighbor on every side. This was the view that Ryland had that night. Was there something to see? Was there something that Ryland saw that day he fell? Or the day before? Or the week before that? Something that someone didn't want him to see? Had he, once again, been a witness to a crime or a secret? Was this why someone cut that rope and let the man who loved Christmas fall to his death?

Tracy sat down on the dusty shingles and stared. "What the hell did you see that day, old buddy? Something that got you murdered?"

* * *

The next morning found Detective Tracy at the law firm of Roberts, Lane, and Ross. He had an appointment with Ryland Reese's lawyer, Adam Levinson. He was hoping to find out what Ryland had in mind in the way of the distribution of his money. It might tell him something. Greed was a killer.

When shown into the office, Mr. Adam Levinson was cordial and directed Tracy to have a seat, which he did. Levinson was on the short side of 6-feet and had eyes that shifted from side to side when he spoke. Tracy couldn't help thinking of every film noir where Edmond O'Brien had graced the big screen.

"I understand, Detective, that you want to know

81

about Ryland Reese's will. I spoke with the kids, and they said to give you carte blanche, so I shall." Levinson slipped on a pair of horn-rimmed glasses and looked at a series of paperwork on his desk. "The kids, of course, inherit the bulk of everything. Which, by the way, is substantial. Ryland didn't like anyone to know, not even his family, but he was a multi-millionaire. Made his money back some time ago while working for a company that manufactured Christmas ornaments. I'm sure you are not surprised by that statement since that particular holiday was his life, so to speak."

Tracy chuckled. He certainly could agree with that statement.

"Ryland perfected a form of Christmas tree tinsel. Up until the 1960's tinsel was made from lead foil. It was banned suddenly when it was discovered that it was harmful and posed a threat to kids and pets. Ryland had a contract with the company and came up with tinsel made from polyvinyl chloride. Even though he let someone else file for the patent, he made the company give him a high dollar amount for the formula. Then he invested the money and turned it into millions with an "s." He always laughed when he told me that tinsel was the most controversial Christmas decoration. Most people hated it. Some threw it on the tree any old way; others placed the stuff on branches in thick bunches, and others had to handset each strand one-by-one. But the damn stuff made him rich. Why he loved Christmas? You tell me, Detective."

Tracy agreed. "If it was me."

Adam Levinson seemed to second the motion. "What else do you need to know, Detective Tracy?"

"I believe what you are saying, Mr. Levinson, is that all of the money after taxes goes to the kids."

"Correct."

"Any other family members inherit? What about the nephew, Jeff Connors? And the other relatives?"

"Ryland did not provide for any, but I happen to know that he told Miss Rachel that she could give any other relatives what she thought was fair. So, it's all up to her. And by the way, nobody knows that little piece of information, Detective."

Tracy thanked Adam Levinson and left the law office. He didn't have any idea what to do next.

* * *

". . .A miniature sleigh and... "
- C.C. Moore

The next morning, Tracy called the kids to Ryland Reese's house for a meeting. It was Sunday. He hated to take them away from their families; the boys were happily married and living nearby in Staten Island, and Rachel was not far. He wasn't sure exactly what he was going to say or how he was going to say it. When everyone was seated at the dining room table, he began, but not where he was hoping to begin. "I'm sorry. I wish I had better news, kids. But I just haven't found a person or persons who would want to harm your father. I believe he was killed for money. Maybe he was even being blackmailed, and he didn't want to tell any of you. I don't know if there is a connection between the threatening letters and his death. I don't know if both acts are one in the same person. But I promise I will keep looking until I find out. A lot of people in Ryland's life may have had a motive. Even as far back as his job with the manufacturing company."

All three Reese children nodded in unison. They were obviously in agreement. It was Ronnie Reese who spoke first. "Nick, did you bring the tape with you? If so, can we watch it again?"

"Sure. I have it here. . ." Tracy slid the tape into the machine and pushed play. The screen came alive with the images of the Christmas party. For three minutes, the four

83

people watched in silence. When it was over, Tracy took the tape back and slipped it in his pocket.

"Were you thinking something, Ronnie? Tell me. Nothing is too small. What you think is unimportant might be the break I need."

Ronnie bit at his lip and looked up at the ceiling. "No, Nick. I was just wondering where everyone was standing. Not that it matters."

Tracy watched as Rachel slipped her arm around her brother and pulled him close. It was a moment for both. Tracy couldn't help but think that Ryland would have been proud of his only daughter. She had a lot of responsibility. There were going to be relatives coming out of the woodwork when the word got out how much Ryland Reese was worth.

Tracy stood and shook hands with the men and hugged Rachel twice. Then he headed to the front door. He could hear the Reese kids talking quietly among themselves. Before he closed the door behind him, he heard a momentary shout, not too loud, and a bit of noise like furniture being pushed aside. And then, there was laughter. Louder this time.

Suddenly, Tracy got a terrible feeling that he had missed something. Did he just get sucker punched by three con artists? Did Ryland Reese really write that note and edit that tape down to the three minutes? Or did someone set up this whole scenario? Maybe three "someones"?

Once back in his apartment, Tracy walked over and threw his keys into the round dish on the table. He then went into the bedroom to change before feeding the menagerie. When all was well, he picked up the phone and called a fellow detective from a neighboring precinct. After ten minutes, Tracy got around to telling him about the case. When he was done, he waited for his take on his findings.

"This sounds like one of the toughest you've ever worked on, Nick. Maybe because you are too close to the subject. You had strong feelings for this Ryland Reese."

"Yeah. So why, all of a sudden, am I suspecting his children of killing him? I don't like it."

"I understand. But you have to ask yourself, 'Why would they plant that letter and that tape?' If they cut that rope and let their father fall to his death, they would let the police conclude it was an accident and then take the money. Why bring you in to investigate? They know how good you are. They would be taking a huge risk that you would get to the truth."

Tracy mulled over this information. "You're right. So, if it isn't the family, then who?" Tracy could hear the shuffling of papers over the phone. He could picture his buddy going to the table.

"Okay, Nick, read me again the note that Ryland Reese left you."

Tracy cleared his throat. "*Away to the window I flew like a flash, tore open the shutters and threw up the sash. . .and he whistled and shouted and called them by name. . .Now Dasher, now Prancer and Vixen. . .On Comet, on Cupid on Donner and Blitzen . . .to the top of the porch, to the top of the wall, now dash away, dash away, dash away all.*"

When he was done, Tracy heard a sharp intake of breath from the other side of the line. "I know this poem, Nick. I had to memorize it in grade school for a Christmas play; I was one of the elves. And you just read me seven reindeer's names, but there are eight. Santa has EIGHT reindeer, Nick."

* * *

"...It must be St. Nick..."
- C.C. Moore

The man wasn't exactly screaming. But his voice was raised just high enough to attract attention. And he was standing, leaning against the brick fireplace. He stuck a pipe in his mouth, but he didn't light it. It looked more like a prop. "No, no. That's not it at all. Ryland Reese helped my wife leave me. He gave her a place to stay in the city and even gave her money for a lawyer, recommended one of his own. It was all so cozy. There was nothing between them, of course, it was strictly a friendship, but it angered me. No man should do that to another man."

"Unless it's necessary, or they deserved it?" Tracy added.

"Maybe. But that's not why I sent him those letters. It wasn't about Julie. No. I sent him those letters because I found out through my work at the City Planning office that they are going to buy out the corner houses on our street, for a lot of money. They are going to offer three times what they are worth. There's a green belt being planned. I tried to buy the house from Ryland, but he didn't want to sell. I told him I would give him 10% more than it appraised for, but he wouldn't budge."

"So, you sent the threatening letters?"

"Yeah. I figured if he thought someone was going to destroy all his Christmas stuff, he might want to move away. Somewhere he wouldn't be bothered. So, I sent the letters. But he still wouldn't. . ."

"So, you cut the safety rope knowing he would fall off the roof and hoping it would kill him."

"No, wait . . .I never cut any rope. I just wanted to buy the house, knowing that in six months, I could triple my investment. I mean what did Ryland care? He would have his money from the house. And besides, I know he was rich. I was over having a beer one day and I saw his bank statement on the desk. He's got more money than God."

"Are you telling me, Mr. Tillman, that you didn't kill Ryland?"

"Of course I didn't kill him. Why would I do that?"

"Well, now that I know about the city buying the land, I'm thinking you knew that the kids would probably put the house up for sale after he was gone. Since you couldn't get Ryland to agree to sell, they would have been easier to deal with."

Bick Tillman walked across the room and took out his pipe tobacco. He stuffed the bowl and then lit it. The aroma instantly filled the room. "I like you, Detective. I don't think you are going to lock up a man for writing some letters. That would make you look like a fool. I've admitted that I wrote them. And I'm curious as to who told you I was the one who sent those notes."

"Ryland Reese."

"When?"

"Yesterday afternoon."

Bick Tillman smiled, verging on a chuckle. And then he frowned. "You're serious, aren't you? Since the man is dead, I am assuming you are speaking metaphorically."

"He left me a message, Mr. Tillman. He suspected that you were the one sending the messages. So, he told Rachel if anything happened to him to give me a letter which led me to a tape of a Christmas party. The letter had a few lines from 'Twas the Night Before Christmas."

"The old kid's poem?"

"Yeah. One of the lines from the poem listed Santa's reindeer. But it wasn't until my buddy pointed out to me that Ryland only listed seven names that I realized which one was missing. I went back to the tape and my list of what everyone was doing at the party and there it was. In black and white."

"What was there, Detective?"

"Ryland knew when I figured out the name of the missing reindeer, I would put it all together. And I did. The name of that reindeer was Dancer. And *you*, Mr. Tillman, on that tape. . .were the dancer."

Tracy stood and started towards the door. He signaled for his man waiting outside. He was about to inform Brick Tillman of his rights and that he was taking him in for questioning in connection with the death of his friend. Maybe Tillman didn't murder anyone. Maybe no one cut that rope. Maybe it really was an accident. Detective Nick Tracy was determined to find out the truth. And he would. But in the meantime…

Merry Christmas in March, Mr. Tillman. Foiled by the brilliant and fanatical mind of Mr. Ryland Reese of Staten Island, New York, the man who loved Christmas.

IT'S ALL ABOUT THE BENJAMINS

PROLOGUE

"If you have a gun, you can rob a bank.
If you have a bank, you can rob everybody."
-B.Maher

Thomas Hamilton III looked down at his nearly empty money drawer; there were twenties, tens, ones, and random change. The money cart behind him was standing empty. It was a Monday morning, and the cash had been delivered to each of the tellers at the Mercantile Bank. And now - all the $100 bills were gone.

Tom looked up at the man who was striding away quickly across the bank floor. Tom could wait no longer. He stuck his finger out, pointing to the man in the bulky trench coat. "Stop him, someone. Stop that man. Hurry. He just robbed the bank."

* * *

Randal Robinson, the security guard for the Mercantile Bank, was just emerging from his morning fog, but Randal was awake enough to hear Thomas Hamilton shouting. He spotted the man in the trench coat who was moving just fast enough to make it out the revolving door. By the time the security guard caught up to the man, he was on the sidewalk that ran parallel to the Mercantile. Robinson reached out and grabbed the man by the collar, his gun at the ready if needed. But the man did little more than squirm beneath his touch. Minimal resistance. The bank guard was relieved. He didn't like to pull out his sidearm. Made him nervous. Like he was a little too close to shooting someone.

Randal turned the man in the trench coat around, shoved him back through the revolving door, and headed inside the bank. There was a small crowd gathering: three customers and the usual gaggle of tellers and bank managers. The front door of the Mercantile Bank was quickly locked, and everyone within the bank's walls, customers and employees alike, were detained. No one was allowed to leave. Everyone stood and watched as Randal hauled the man in the trench coat to the back room.

It would be only moments before the police would arrive, and, all the while, everyone was congratulating the brave security guard as the man in the coat proclaimed his innocence, over and over again. Nobody searched the man. Nobody listened to the man's protests. It was better to wait for the police and let them do all the hard work.

However, when the NYPD officer arrived, there was a problem. After searching the man in the bulky trench coat, the nice policeman discovered there was no money to be found other than $43.00 in loose bills and six rolls of quarters, six rolls of dimes, and six rolls of nickels, all still in Mercantile wrappers. No crisp one-hundred-dollar bills. Every one Thomas Hamilton had in the money cart since the man in the trench coat was only his third customer of the day; the first man cashed a meager check while the second made a small deposit of $80.

"This thug here must have taken at least $25 thousand," Tom Hamilton declared out loud.

Officer Leonard Newton of the New York Police Department merely nodded in the teller's direction. He understood, but he really didn't. "So, Mr. Hamilton, where is the note demanding the money? It's not on this gentleman's person. I've searched him thoroughly."

Tom Hamilton III glowered at the holdup man, who was sweating profusely. "There were two notes, Officer. One asking for dimes, nickels, and quarters. Six rolls each. And one asking for all of the $100 bills in my drawer and in my cart or. . .or else he would shoot me. This man took the holdup note with him, but I think the other note is sitting on my counter. I was so shook. . ."

Officer Newton turned to the bank manager, a Mr. Ralph Emerson. "What about the closed-circuit camera? Can I get a copy of the tape?"

Ralph Emerson went pale. "The CCTV was not turned on. Alice Long normally turns on the switch when she comes in. But she was late this morning; she didn't get to the closed circuit."

Officer Newton looked over the gathered individuals. "Okay, everyone. So, we have a man here in a trench coat with nothing but rolls of coins on him. A CCTV not functioning. A missing hold-up note. And twenty-five thousand dollars that seems to have vanished into thin air. Can anyone offer an explanation as to what happened?"

The bank teller, Tom Hamilton, was starting to pace back and forth. His face was red. "You have to search him again, Officer. Did you check the linings of his coat? Something is wrong here. He must have the money and the note on him somewhere. He didn't get far out of the door or . . ."

Bank guard Randal Robinson butted in. "I know what you are thinking, Tom, but he was no more than six or seven steps out of that revolving door. How could he have handed the money off without my seeing? We can check the tape from the outside cameras; they are always on, but I'm telling you that he didn't have the time to hand off anything. Unless. . ."

Officer Newton took the handcuffs off the man in the trench coat as everyone turned to stare at the man who now had a name - Johnny Benjamin. Benjamin threw up his hands and his eyebrows at the same time. "I told you I was innocent. I didn't take any money. You have all made a big mistake."

Tom Hamilton glared at the robber with the eyes of fire. He looked as if he were going to punch Benjamin in the face. "I know you handed off that money. Don't you dare smile at me. The police are going to figure out how you did it, and then you are going to jail. You are a thief."

A few minutes later out in the bank lobby, everyone, including all employees, were searched thoroughly in case Benjamin had somehow found a way to pass off the money to someone inside the Mercantile. All of the teller drawers were counted and documented. When everyone was released the bank employees all turned and watched as Johnny Benjamin received a strict warning from Officer Newton and then walked out the front door of the bank, a free man. Could anyone explain what just happened? No. But maybe there was someone, somewhere, who could.

* * *

*"Banks are places that will lend you money
if you can prove you don't need it."*
- B. Hope

Detective Nick Tracy yawned and stretched at this desk, trying to wake up, unaware that he was about to be handed a case that would keep him awake at night. Maybe that was why he almost didn't hear his office door opening. He took a wild stab as to who was walking over the threshold. Chief Patton smiled, showing straight white teeth and a bit of chocolate doughnut from the break room pastry selection.

"Good morning, Detective Tracy. I know you have a full caseload and you are busy, but. . ." (There was always a *but,* and everything said before it was always bull crap.) ". . .I need you to take a look at a burglary over at the Mercantile Bank. It's technically not a robbery, as the man who reportedly stole the money does not have it. No one can find the money." Chief Patton threw a manilla file on Tracy's desk before he continued.

"It's all in there. The bare bones: when the bank opened yesterday morning, it was robbed. The security guard grabbed the man after he had taken six steps outside the front door. One of our guys, Newton, over in robbery, arrived and searched the man who was wearing a large trench coat. In fact, he searched everyone and everywhere in the bank. But there was no money. The teller said the perp took the demand note with him and that the man put the note inside his coat with the money. The note was easily disposed of outside the bank, but the fact that there was no money, well. . . Robinson had to let the man go. We were going to bring this Benjamin in for questioning but after checking him for priors, there are none by the way, I doubt we can find any reason to detain him."

Tracy was thinking to himself that each sentence was worse than the last one when Chief Patton put on his serious face.

"That's why I need you, Tracy. Find out how this guy pulled this off. I want to nail this Benjamin."

Tracy took the manilla envelope and opened the contents. He then turned back to his superior, who looked like he was ready to run away after dumping the case in Tracy's lap.

"Chief, is this the Mercantile bank over on 8th Avenue?"

"You know it?"

"Yeah. I know it. Dated a girl once who worked there. Nice girl. . ."

"Just figure out what this Benjamin guy did with the money, Tracy. I'm going back out that door to my office, and you're not. You're going to 8th Avenue."

* * *

"Money is like the sixth sense.
You can't make use of the other five without it."
- S. Maugham

Most New York City detectives liked to start an investigation with the perpetrator or *suspected* perp. Nick Tracy liked to begin at the beginning - at the scene of the crime. The Mercantile Bank on 8th was still reeling from the robbery the day before. Tracy went straight to the manager's office and asked if everyone involved in the incident could please meet him in the conference room in five. Everyone complied. No exceptions. Tracy knew what he was up against. This crime had vast textured layers, and he was a day behind.

When everyone was assembled, Tracy began. First up, the bank teller, Mr. Thomas Hamilton III."Tell me everything from the beginning, Mr. Hamilton. Starting with the moment you walked into the bank yesterday morning."

Thomas Hamilton had dark brown hair and matching eyes. He was tall and thin, in an Ichabod Crane sort of way. He took in all that was Detective Nick Tracy and then started to speak. Slowly at first. "Okay. I came in through the employees' entrance, in the back. Randy, Mr. Robinson our security guard, let me in. He let us all in. After coffee, I went to my station and started unloading my cash cart. Everyone was talking about their weekend. It was a very congenial morning. I almost had all the money loaded into my drawer. I was talking to the teller on my right, Ginny/teller number two, when Randy unlocked the front door, and the first customer came to my window. He made a small deposit. And then a second customer came almost immediately on his heels. Cashed a small check for $80. I gave him four $20 bills. The third customer, a man in a large trench coat, then stepped up to my window and handed me a note. He said he needed the change for his kid's birthday party; the boy and his friends were going to an arcade. The note listed six rolls of quarters, six rolls of dimes, and six rolls of nickels. He gave me the exact amount of cash to cover the coins."

"Was there anyone else standing in line behind him?" Tracy inquired.

"No."

"And did he say anything else?"

"Not until after I gave him the wrapped coins. Then he said something like, 'Oh, one more thing.' And then he shoved another note under the bars on my window. I looked at the note, and I couldn't believe it. The note said, *'Give me your $100 bills, all of them, or I will blow your head off with the gun I have under the counter. After I'm out the door, count to ten before you say a word. Don't try to be a hero. I won't let you.'*

"And then you gave him all of the 100s in your drawers from the cash cart?"

"Yes. And I kept quiet for a few seconds. But then I just got mad and screamed out, 'Stop that guy! He robbed the bank!' or something like that. I can't remember exactly. It happened so fast."

"And I understand that the man in the trench coat took the demand note with him."

"Yes, he did. But he didn't take the note about the coins."

"Okay, I'll take a look at that note in a minute. Now

tell me what happened next, Mr. Hamilton."

"Simple, Detective. Randy grabbed the man out front of the bank and held him until one of your officers got here and searched him. By that time, there was no money, no note, no nothing. Just the rolls of coins, which I'm thinking now was only to make him look innocent when we couldn't find any money."

Tracy turned to Randal Robinson. The security guard was smiling.

"You don't have to ask, Detective. I will tell you everything. When Thomas screamed, I jumped into action. The suspect was almost through the revolving door with his hands in his pocket. I didn't consider my safety for one minute. I unsnapped my holster with my gun inside but didn't draw. I just grabbed for the man's collar with my left hand in case I needed to draw my weapon with my right. But he didn't struggle. When I apprehended him, he was about six to eight steps out the door onto the sidewalk out front. That's when I hauled his ass back into the bank and into the room here. Like I said, he didn't struggle. We called for police assistance, and Officer Newton showed up. He took our statements and searched the perp, but he didn't find a thing on the man. Just the wrapped coins. Ten-four that." Mr. Randal Robinson had obviously watched a few too many cop shows.

"Okay, everyone. I got the picture. Only, the money must be somewhere." Tracy turned back to the security guard. "Was there anyone outside on the sidewalk by the time you got to the robber?"

"Yes. The sidewalk was full of people. I didn't see him talking to anyone or giving anybody anything."

Tracy nodded his understanding and then dismissed everyone except for the bank manager. Ralph Emerson was a short, stalky man who looked every inch the part. Tracy didn't trust bankers. He wasn't sure why, but it might have something to do with his uncles and their philosophy. *When*

*you need to borrow money, Nicky, the mob is a better bet than
some bank. The mob may threaten you, like if you don't pay, they
will break something. What? Break my legs? Is that all? I'll
settle for broken legs over taking my house and ruining my credit
any day. Where do I sign?*

Tracy addressed manager Emerson. "I need to
know, sir, if you have checked everywhere in this bank for
the money: garbage cans, back offices, the men's room,
other tellers' cages, the dock. . ."

"Of course, Detective," Emerson said with an air of
defense. "This isn't the first time we've been robbed. We
know the drill around here. And I am a very intelligent and
astute man who would never leave one rock unturned.
Money is money. And the Mercantile Bank pays me to
babysit its employees and make sure no money goes
missing. And I do my job very well."

"I'm sure you do, sir. I would never question your
ability, but I had to ask. Now, I am leaving to question
Johnny Benjamin. I will find out what happened to your
money, but I will tell you that I am beginning to believe
that there was a second party to this heist. Someone outside
of the bank to take the money."

* * *

*"Money if it does not bring happiness,
will at least help you be miserable in comfort."*
- H. Brown

The Benjamin apartment, around the corner from
the Mercantile Bank, was modest but clean and tidy. At the
moment, Mr. and Mrs. Johnny Benjamin were sitting on the
chenille sofa. They looked more like brother and sister than
husband and wife. Same size, similar facial features. Their
hands were folded in their laps, prim and proper as if they
were entertaining their local priest. But Detective Tracy
was no priest. He had been an altar boy at one time, but

those days were long behind him. *Deo gratias.*

"So, let me get this straight, Mr. Benjamin. You went into the bank yesterday morning to get your son some coins for the arcade games at his birthday party, which was last night, and you ended up as a suspect in a robbery?"

"Yes, Detective."

"And you have no idea what led the teller of the Mercantile Bank to suspect you of robbing him of twenty-five grand?"

"No, Detective."

Mrs. Benjamin spoke for the first time. She was timid, shy, and attractive. "This whole thing is, like, just a mistake, Detective. My Johnny would never like do anything like rob a bank. He is, like, a good husband and father. Sure, we need money. Like, who doesn't? But we don't, like, resort to robbery."

Tracy was just thinking to himself that these two were really good at this innocent act, when John Jr., all of nine years old, burst through the front door with a couple of buddies by his side. Tracy decided to do a little questioning. John Jr. squirmed a bit by his father's side, but he kept his eyes steady, at least steady for a fidgety nine-year-old. "So, how was your arcade visit last night? Did you and your buddies have a good time?"

The young boy beamed as if recalling the spectacular night in wide-screen and technicolor. "Yeah. It was super cool. One of my friends got high-score on that new Pac-Man game that just came out. It was really cool."

After a few more questions, Tracy had heard enough. "Okay, thanks, John Jr. And happy birthday."

A puzzled look crossed the boy's eyes. He yelled back over his shoulder as he ran to join his friends. "Yeah, thanks, but it's not my birthday. I was born in June."

Tracy turned back to the father, who jumped in quickly. "Sorry, Detective. Don't know why I said that. Guess I was just nervous."

* * *

"The safest way to double your money
is to fold it over and put it in your pocket."
- J.Mason

The next morning, Tracy was back in the Mercantile Bank. He had requested an opportunity to view the CCTV footage from the front sidewalk on the morning of the robbery since there was no CC tape for the inside of the bank. Mr. Ralph Emerson had provided said tape and the two men were viewing it together. When they reached the moments following the robbery, it was apparent that there were more than just a few people milling around on the sidewalk when Johnny Benjamin came through the revolving door. In a matter of seconds, before Randal Robinson grabbed for his collar, Benjamin passed very near to no less than sixteen people. Because of the chilly weather, all were wearing large coats. All appeared to be men except for one female-looking individual who brushed by very close to Benjamin, close enough for him to pass a stack of bills beneath his coat. (Tracy had experimented a bit and found that $25,000 in $100 bills is less than half as tall as an ink pen.) Unfortunately, even after a decent look, none of the individuals were recognizable; they could have been anyone in the city of New York.

Tracy sat back in his chair. A dead end. There was no way to link Benjamin to any one of those men on the sidewalk. Not unless he tracked down every friend, acquaintance, and co-worker that Benjamin had ever had contact with. And even then, there was no guarantee. A haystack with a needle.

Tracy turned to Emerson, who was just putting away the CCTV tape. "Is Alice Long here today, Mr. Emerson?"

"Yes, she is Detective. Do you want to speak with

her?"

Tracy nodded a yes, and the bank manager went to fetch Miss Long for questioning. It was only a matter of minutes before he returned with a cute young woman who looked nervous and anxious. She bit her lower lip as she sat down in a chair near Tracy. But not too near. "So, Miss Long. On the morning of the robbery, you were late for work. You didn't get in the bank until Randal, the security guard, opened the door for you. It was after the robbery had taken place. At that time, you turned on the closed-circuit TV inside the bank. Am I correct so far?"

"Yes, sir."

"Could you please tell me why you were late for work?"

"Yes. I received a call from my daughter's school. I had dropped her off at the bus stop only a half hour before. The caller said that my daughter was in the nurse's office sick and would I please come pick her up right away."

"Was it a woman's voice on the phone?"

"Yes."

"And what happened when you got to your daughter's school?"

"The nurse said she never called. And my daughter was in class."

Tracy turned to Ralph Emerson. "Would you mind leaving us alone, Mr. Emerson?"

With a visible huff, the bank manager stood and made his way to the door. He didn't look back. When Tracy and Alice Long were alone, Tracy proceeded. "I want you to answer my next question truthfully, Miss Long. This is just between you and I, for now. But the truth is important. Do you know Johnny Benjamin?"

"Yes. He is a client here at Mercantile. He comes in frequently. Always to my window."

"I meant, do you *know* him - away from the bank? On a personal basis?"

Alice Long squirmed again in her seat. The lip-biting took on renewed vigor. "Yes, Detective. I've had a few drinks with him after hours. The office where he works is not far from here. I'm a widow, and sometimes I get lonely for male companionship. Just talk and a few beers."

"And does Mr. Benjamin have your phone number?"

"Yes."

"What about Mrs. Benjamin? Do you know her also?"

"I've only seen her once when she came in to cash a check, not at my window."

Tracy stood, and Alice Long jumped to her feet in response. "Okay, thank you, Miss Long. If I have any more questions, I will contact you. But that is all for now."

The teller left the room. She couldn't get out the door fast enough. Was this an affair between Johnny Benjamin and Alice Long? Or just a flirtation? Either way it left an opening in Tracy's mind and a big question.

* * *

The office building where Johnny Benjamin worked as a file clerk was within walking distance from the Mercantile Bank. Tracy made it in three minutes. He spent a bit of time talking with a few of Benjamin's co-workers. Benjamin was home sick, they said. After a few strategic questions, Tracy ascertained that Johnny Benjamin was short on cash. One loose-lipped blabbermouth even told him that Johnny was visited by some shady characters looking for a payoff. Loan sharks or something. Later, someone said they were there collecting gambling debts. According to everyone Tracy spoke with, it appeared that Benjamin liked the dice games uptown and had a gambling problem, big time.

This case was getting more and more interesting

and complex as time went on. Johnny Benjamin appeared to be a smooth operator with money problems and a nice little way to make $25,000 in cash disappear into thin air.

* * *

*"Money is better than poverty,
if only for financial reasons." - W. Allen*

Back at the precinct, Tracy made a quick call to Ralph Emerson, the bank manager. "Benjamin was searched very thoroughly, Detective. I mean, I stood there and watched the procedure, never moved a muscle. I would say that your officer did everything short of a strip search. I mean, there's only so many places a guy can hide that much cash."

"Okay, Mr. Emerson. Thank you. And just another quick question, how long has Alice Long been employed at your bank?"

"Eight years, I believe."

"And how trustworthy is she? Have you ever known any incident where she lied?"

"Never. Alice is very loyal to the Mercantile. We are like a family here, Detective. That is why I gave her the job of turning on the CCTV camera each morning. I knew I could rely on her."

"Okay, Mr. Emerson. Thank you again for the information. I will get back to you."

With that, Tracy hung up the phone and grabbed his coat. He was headed back to a neighborhood that was going to prove more fruitful than he originally thought.

* * *

In Johnny and Paula Benjamin's apartment house, every door Detective Tracy knocked on reinforced the age-old adage: good news may travel fast, but bad news spreads like wildfire. Everyone in the building had heard about the bank robbery and how their neighbor Johnny Benjamin was under suspicion. Good stuff. Something to chew on besides Mr. Richfield's lost cat and Mrs. White's late-night rendezvous with 5C's brother-in-law. And everyone wanted to talk about Johnny Benjamin. And the Mrs.

"He is a bit standoffish.... He is a hoarder… She spoils that Johnny Jr. rotten…There's a gambling problem… She works at a grocery store down the block…He goes out at night gambling…I don't think he is the bank robber type, but you never know…He's got a mean streak somewhere underneath that nice exterior…He rescued my dog; he's a hero… He's a jerk, haul him into the station…"

By the time Tracy left the old apartment building, he was nowhere near the truth about the Benjamins. However, he did feel as if he knew them better. They were a mystery. But not one that couldn't be unraveled. He headed to the grocery store where Paula Benjamin worked as a cashier. Maybe he could find some answers there. But it was doubtful.

* * *

"Money in the bank is like toothpaste.
Easy to get out, hard to put back."
- E. Wilson

The small neighborhood grocery store was packed with locals who didn't want to wait in line at the big chain stores. Paula Benjamin wasn't working that day, but she was scheduled for the next day. A big, burly man by the name of Abbott took Tracy into the back room, away from prying eyes and big ears, and told him to have a seat on a crate of cereal boxes still to be unpacked. Tracy did as he was told. Mr. Rochester Abbott was the size of a mountain.

"What do you want to know about Paula, Detective? She in trouble?"

"I don't know yet, Mr. Abbott. Can you tell me if Paula Benjamin is a good employee? Do you know her well? And does she have money problems?"

Abbott wiped the perspiration from his massive forehead with the back of his sleeve. The shirt was a 3X-large. "Yes. Yes. And I don't know."

"Okay. Let me put it another way. Has she asked for a raise lately? Has she indicated to you that she needs more money to make ends meet at home? That sort of thing?"

"She hasn't asked for a raise, but she did ask for some time off to take care of some personal matters. Does that count?"

"Maybe. Do you know what those personal matters were in particular?"

"No. I may run this store, but I keep to myself. And I stay out of my employees' business. Real life takes place off stage, Detective. You can get caught back there, and then you're in too deep. So, I keep away from personal problems."

Tracy thanked the store manager and was just heading to the front door when someone, a short red-headed woman with glasses and a pair of shallow lips, grabbed for his arm. "Wait a second, cop. I might have some information that you will want to hear. I know you are asking about Paula. And I know why you're asking. But what the big guy back there doesn't know is that Paula and I trade secrets. . .and she is in big trouble. There are some gambling debts that aren't going away. And the interest is piling on and compounding daily."

"Yes, ma'am. I know. I've heard about Johnny Benjamin's nasty little habit. Gambling isn't . . ."

"Wait a second, gumshoe. You've got it all wrong here. Those nasty little gambling debts aren't Johnny's.

They are Paula's."

* * *

Tracy used the pay phone in the back of the small grocery store. He placed a call to Alice Long at Mercantile Bank. He had only one question, "Would you recognize Paula Benjamin's voice if you heard it?" The answer: "No."

* * *

*"Banking may be a career from which
no man really recovers."
- J.K. Galbraith*

It was a good crowd for a weekday. The regulars at the Blue Note Tavern were just shuffling in when Tracy found Johnny Benjamin behind a scotch and water at the bar. The chrome stool he was perched on had seen better years. Benjamin looked tired and maybe a little bit sheepish, like a boy who knew his mom was right about the missing cookies. He didn't see Tracy approaching.

"If I might have a word with you, Mr. Benjamin?"

By the time Benjamin put a name with the voice, he was already in full swivel. He stood to his feet and looked at Tracy with eyes that were bloodshot. He hadn't spilled a single drop of the scotch and soda. "Sure. Let's go to the back booth. No, over there in the corner."

Apparently, Benjamin didn't want the regulars at the Blue Note Tavern to know he was being questioned by a big city detective. Maybe they hadn't heard. Some drunk yelled out that he had a tip for Johnny, the gray in the fifth at Belmont, as the two men approached the booth, which was about the time the piano player flipped his sheet music and began a rendition of a Tony Bennett classic. Once they slid in the red vinyl booth held together with duct tape and

105

spit, Tracy was ready.

"What can you tell me about your wife's gambling problem? How deep is she into the loan sharks?"

Benjamin looked like he was about to deny it, but thought better of it. "It's nothing, Detective. Really. I can handle it. Sometimes Paula gets carried away. Forgets herself. She is usually better. She can make it rain. But not this time. A dry streak of bad luck."

"Yeah, I've heard that can happen."

"Oh, come on. You weren't thinking that I robbed the Mercantile to pay off her gambling debts, were you? 'Cause that's not the case."

"No? Then why *did* you rob the Mercantile?"

"Oh no, you don't, Detective. Stop trying to put words in my mouth. I didn't rob that bank. And you can't prove that I did. So, we are basically wasting each other's valuable time."

"It's not a waste of time, Mr. Benjamin. I'm a homicide detective, but I've taken a real liking to this case. And I am going to see it through. You say you didn't rob the bank. I say you did. So, here's what I am asking. Come to the station tomorrow afternoon around 1 o'clock. Both you and the Mrs. I don't want to have to send a squad car after you. Your neighbors don't need any more fodder."

Tracy stood and started toward the door. After a few steps he turned back. "Remember, Mr. Benjamin. . .1 o'clock tomorrow. You and the Mrs. Don't be late."

And with that, Tracy left the small bar and passed beneath the blinking neon light that declared this was: THE BL E NOTE TAV N.

*"If you owe the bank $100 that is your problem.
If you owe the bank $100 million, that's the bank's
problem." - J.P. Getty*

Everyone was seated around the table in the interrogation room. Chief Patton, Tracy, Rob Davidson, the head of the robbery division, Johnny Benjamin, and Paula Benjamin. Nice congenial group with nothing more in common than a sweet little robbery over on 8th Avenue that had made $25 grand disappear.

Tracy had the floor. "Mr. and Mrs. Benjamin, you have been called in today to answer allegations that you staged the robbery of the Mercantile Bank over on 8th Avenue. I have not been able to recover the money or the note from the robbery. I believe that you have already disposed of both. It's my contention that you paid off Paula's gambling debts with the $25,000 and intentionally destroyed the holdup note. I'm giving you a chance to tell me the truth."

It was Paula Benjamin who jumped in. "This is, like, absurd, Detective Tracy. Who do you think you are? Like, we are law-abiding citizens. I still don't understand why you suspect my Johnny of even robbing the bank."

"So, you are denying any involvement in this crime, Mrs. Benjamin? You didn't call Alice Long to delay her by telling her to pick up her daughter right away at school? And you didn't take possession of the stolen money outside the Mercantile that morning disguised in an oversized trench coat and a hat?"

"No. None of that. I'm denying it all. The whole thing is, like, ridiculous. You have no money. No proof."

His wife's protests seemed to prompt the location of Johnny Benjamin's tongue. "You are making a big mistake, Detective. We don't want to make a statement. I want to call my brother-in-law. He's a lawyer, not a good one, but better than sitting here being accused of something I didn't do with no representation."

"Alright. The boys are going to read you your rights and then book you. Then you can make that call."

* * *

Later that afternoon, Tracy stopped in at the Mercantile Bank. He had a brief conversation with Ralph Emerson and explained that the Benjamins had been booked for suspicion of robbery. He promised he would keep Mr. Emerson posted as to the progress of the arrest. The bank manager was grateful for the information and thanked Tracy for his assistance.

"I understand this wasn't even your department, Detective. I hear you work in homicide. But I'm thankful you stepped in. Our security guard, Randy, is useless. I've tried to replace him several times. I mean, the man is a bona fide Barney Fife with endless boring stories about his collection. I mean, who collects porcelain pigs? Really? Porcelain Pigs?"

Tracy shifted his weight to the other foot. "Look, I was happy to help, Mr. Emerson. And I don't know if we can get a conviction to stick. Let's wait and see what happens. But I have a feeling your $25,000 is gone."

After a few more "thank yous" and "we are gratefuls" trailing after him, Tracy left the bank manager's office on his way back to a mound of paperwork at the precinct. As he was leaving the lobby of the bank, he stopped for a moment; a feeling of unrest, like something was wrong, passed over him. But what could be wrong? And that's when he took a good look at the tellers' windows and their close proximity to one another. You couldn't throw a dollar bill without hitting one of them. Ginny Atkins was on Thomas Hamilton's right, within an arm's length. The money was all the same. The only thing

108

different was the tellers. If she could. . .

Tracy did a 180-degree turn and retraced his steps. He returned to the bank manager's office and found Ralph Emerson shuffling through some papers on his desk trying to look busy. He wasn't succeeding. "Mr. Emerson, could you please pull the tellers' transaction sheets for the day of the robbery? All of the tellers?"

"Of course, Detective. Just give me a minute, and I will have them for you. And do you mind if I ask if there is a particular reason why you want them?"

"I can't say yet, Mr. Emerson. It is just a hunch. And please make sure I have all of them."

"Why wouldn't I make sure, Detective? You said all of them, and that's what you will get. I'm not incompetent, you know. Now, if you will excuse me."

With that, Ralph Emerson rose from his desk and left the room with a backward glance, his face contorted into an unhappy grimace. When Emerson returned, he was holding a folder containing the material Tracy had requested. Reluctantly, at first, the banker turned over the folder to Tracy. *Why was Mr. Emerson reluctant?* And when Tracy thumbed through the papers and read what was written there, he knew. It was all so simple. Like taking candy from a baby. . .or a porcelain-pig-collecting Barney Fife.

* * *

"A banker is a fellow who lends you his umbrella when the sun is shining but wants it back the minute it begins to rain." - M. Twain

Tracy and his cousin Mary were at the corner table of a sweet little café in the Village for a very early dinner. Neither had found time for lunch that day. Busy schedules. And they were hungry. The last of the sun was playing at the edge of the day when the entrée had been cleared, and dessert was on the way. Mary turned to Tracy with an inquisitive look. "Okay, Detective, do you mind if I take a guess at this one?"

There are those who have the "upper hand," and there are those who have the "*unfair* upper hand." And Mary Rosetti was the kind of woman who had the unfair kind. Tracy knew that for the rest of his life he would never be able to utter the word "no" when this woman asked him for, well, anything. He wiped away the last traces of flounder with his napkin.

"Be my guest, cousin. I've given you all the facts."

"Okay. The Benjamins pulled off the robbery together. Johnny Benjamin struck up a friendship with Alice Long to get her phone number so that Paula Benjamin could call Alice with a phony story that delayed Alice's arrival at the bank, which delayed the start of the inside closed-circuit camera. Johnny Benjamin gave Thomas Hamilton the note for the rolls of coins first in case he got caught it would look like that was his reason for being in the bank. Then, all Paula had to do was wait outside disguised as a man in a trench coat, and Johnny passed the stack of 100s *and* the note to her on the sidewalk. When no one could find any money on Johnny, they let him go, and Johnny and Paula went home and paid off her gambling debts so there wouldn't be any traceable big deposits in their account."

"That was my theory."

"So now let me guess. That was your theory until you realized that something was wrong. You mentioned the teller next to Hamilton. Some woman named Ginny? And the bank manager's reluctance to hand over the day's transactions. Were they. . .? Okay, Detective. I can see it on your face. What am I missing?"

The waitress was just delivering Finch's famous cheesecake. Tracy let her set down the plate and two forks. "Okay, let me start by saying every one of those statements you just made is wrong."

"Every single one? Starting back with the Benjamins robbing the bank?"

"Yes."

"Okay, Detective. Give it to me from the beginning."

"Okay, it's like this. The whole heist was so simple that it borders on genius. Hamilton took delivery of his money that morning, settled everything into his station, and simply sat back and waited for his first customer, who was a total stranger, to come through the door. When the first customer's transaction was complete, he waited for the second customer to step up to his window. He handed the stack of $100 bills to the man second in line. The accomplice then walked out of the bank with the money in his coat and passed by one Johnny Benjamin, who was entering the bank and had just become the perfect patsy. When Johnny Benjamin showed Hamilton the note and asked for change for his son's party, all Hamilton had to do was take care of the simple transaction, be patient for a few seconds, wait until Benjamin was almost to the door, and then yell, "Stop that man." But not too soon. Hamilton wanted to give Benjamin enough time, so it looked as if he went outside and passed the money and the note to someone on the bank sidewalk. Later, after Benjamin was apprehended and everyone else in the bank was searched, and no money was found, we all assumed Benjamin did just that. There were so many people on the outside tape. All wearing coats. But Hamilton's accomplice was long gone. They probably met up later and divided the $25 grand."

"So, the money was already out of the bank when Johnny Benjamin walked up to Hamilton's window?"

"Yes. Benjamin told the truth all along. He never gave Hamilton a robbery note. And he never robbed anyone."

"But who called and delayed Alice Long? It was a female voice."

"One thing I didn't think about, didn't know that I had to, was the fact that there was a Mrs. Hamilton somewhere. She apparently made the call for her husband."

"Wow, what an interesting case. What put you onto the teller Hamilton?"

"When I went back to Ralph Emerson, the bank manager, and asked for the logs for the day, I realized that there was something wrong. Hamilton made one mistake. He stated that Benjamin was his third customer. The first customer made a small deposit, and the second customer cashed a check for $80. The first amount matched Hamilton's cash drawer total. But there was no sign of the second transaction, the four $20 bills. In all the confusion, no one had bothered to look at Hamilton's recording sheet and match it up with his cash drawer. It was there in black and white. Where were the four $20 bills that Hamilton stated to the police he gave to his second customer? His drawer should have been short the $80. Which meant there was no second customer transaction. Why had Hamilton lied? To cover?"

"Hamilton almost got away with it."

"Yes. He did. He was smart. And he would have pulled off the perfect robbery if I hadn't looked at the missing money the way I do a homicide. The 'what if' factor. Go back to the last person to see someone alive or, in this case, the last person to actually handle the money."

Cousin Mary nodded and smiled as she stole the next to last bite of cheesecake before Tracy knew what was happening. "Nice work, cousin Nick," she said as she wrapped her lips around the creamy cake clinging to her fork. "Thomas Hamilton was greedy…he was obviously tempted by all that money he handled every day. What does that funny little comedienne Jackie Mason say, *Money is not the most important thing in the world; love is.*

Fortunately, I love money.'"

Tracy threw back his head and laughed before filling his own fork with the last of Finch's specialty, strawberry cheesecake. He made a suggestion. "Why don't we walk home? I know it's a bit far but. . ."

Mary stood and threw her coat around her shoulders with a bit of dramatics. "Say no more, Detective. I am willing to brave the thugs out there if you are. I feel pretty safe beside the number one Detective in New York City."

WINE, CHEESE...AND DAGGERS (ARE BACK IN STYLE)

PROLOGUE

"Style is an overrated necessity."
- H.D. Thoreau

It was 9:29 p.m., and the movie house was just letting out in Southampton, New York - a quiet little hamlet on the great mass of land known as Long Island. It was a nice crowd for a Wednesday night, even though everyone in town said that the up-and-coming 1980s would probably be the death of the tiny theater. Pity. But for now, it was a great way to pass an evening. As the sea of cars was moving onto the main road, a classic Ford Thunderbird was merging with the rest of the movie crowd. Inside the Ford, two people were laughing and enjoying themselves immensely.

Emanuel and Angelica Castor were brother and sister and best friends out of a need for self-preservation. Angelica was a tall and willowy twenty-six-year-old with long dark auburn hair and the kind of complexion an English lass would envy. She was not beautiful, but she possessed a certain style. Angelica's brother Emanuel, two years older, was dark-complected like his late mother, with black hair and brown eyes that sparkled when he smiled. He was tall and heavier than Angelica but carried his weight well.

After parking the car along a row of village stores, the two Castor siblings strolled leisurely down the sidewalk and into a small coffee shop, part of a ritual they performed each Wednesday night. They loved movies, yes, but more than that, these moments away from the big house gave them an escape, creating time when they could talk with complete abandon about their lives, their loves and, of course, their "father." This was their existence, and Angelica and Emanuel were happy with it, but they had come by this life quite by accident.

Twenty years before, Rosalina Gomez Castor had died, leaving her two young children in the care of the wealthy man she had married on a whim, Peter Ivan Castor. Angelica and Emanuel had been the baggage their mother had brought into the marriage, but Peter Castor had accepted this fact and quickly adopted both Angelica and Emanuel. With their mother's sudden death, the two young siblings had become inseparable, clinging to each other out of necessity as they were forced to fall into the routine of their stepfather's everyday life. Each night, once their stepfather was taken care of and all was quiet in the house, they would find something to do to occupy their time. When they were younger, it had been homework, friends, dates, and later Literature classes at a nearby junior college. Today, there were more pressing matters; although the two siblings had become content with their lives and resigned to the fact that they would be their wealthy father's companions for some time, they

As the Castors made their way to their usual table at the back of the small coffee shop, they waved to their favorite waiter, who was already crossing the wooden floor with their standing Wednesday night order of pie and coffee. Once seated, the brother and sister chatted about the movie, analyzing their favorite scenes. When their plates were empty and the apple pie mere crumbs, they bid the owner of the small café goodbye and left the building. As usual, the drive home was uneventful. When they finally pulled onto the long driveway that led up to the mansion, they were tired and ready for bed.

But tonight, things were to be different. Very different. There was going to be a tragedy awaiting the two Castor siblings as they entered the house and proceeded into the foyer. While they had been enjoying themselves, laughing, and talking, their stepfather had suffered a terrible fate. Of course, how could they have known? And yet, the coming chain of events was going to change their lives in ways that no one could have predicted and for longer than... how do the poets put it? Oh yes, *forever and a day.*

* * *

"Trends change. Style endures. . ."
- C. Chanel

It was a house. No, a mansion, in the Hamptons, not far from the now notorious residence where the discovery of millionaire John Roth's body had created weeks of newspaper headlines. This house was equally as appointed as the Howell mansion: ten thousand square feet of architectural beauty with eight bedrooms, nine bathrooms, a study, and a dining room that could accommodate twenty

and more sitting rooms than one could count. Exquisite.
Except. . .

At the present moment, the owner of the mansion
was nothing more than a dead man lying in the front foyer
with an emerald-handled dagger in his chest and blood
soiling his white nightshirt spun from the finest of cotton,
Egyptian, no doubt. Not a pretty sight.

* * *

Angelica Castor stared at her father lying there so
still and lifeless. And then she turned to her brother
Emanuel standing nearby. Did he have the same thoughts?
Of course, he did. Angelica grabbed for his arm and held
tightly. She hated all of these men scurrying around like
cockroaches nibbling at scraps of food left so carelessly
behind. It offended her sense of order. No, she didn't like it
one bit.

And then there was the head investigator. Earlier
one of the men on the forensic team had thrown out a few
reassuring words of praise for this homicide detective on
loan from some Manhattan Precinct. Something like,
"Detective Tracy will help us get to the bottom of this,
Miss. Don't worry. He was a big help on the Roth case."

Like everyone else in the Hamptons, Angelica knew
all the gory details about the discovery of John Roth's
body. It was a scandal within a murder, all tied up in a very
sinister bow at the Howell mansion only a few blocks
away. Angelica made a face at the thought of those
Howells who would probably be calling on her and her
brother to offer condolences. What they would really be
doing is snooping. They were always meddling in
everyone's business, or so her father would say – *used* to
say, past tense. That sounded so strange. The Howells
would no doubt pat her on the hand over and over and say
something silly like, "Don't worry, dear. "But Angelica

117

Castor did worry. And she would doubt. Everything. But for now, she would go along with the program, be a good girl, and keep quiet. She took a few steps back and watched the team examine her father's body.

Peter Castor had been a small, frail, sick man in his late 60s with gray hair and a wrinkled face that was covered with dark spots amid the random group of freckles. He was not an especially attractive man. In fact, when Angelica and her brother stared at the photo of their beautiful mother, they tried their best to figure out what she possibly could have seen in this man. Of course, there was the money. And now, here he was lying in the entryway foyer just beyond the staircase. It was obvious to anyone who bothered to look that her father was stabbed somewhere in the house and left to die there on the floor of his palatial home wearing his flimsy nightshirt, his arms and legs splayed out in all directions. Angelica mulled over the humiliation she knew her father would have felt. The indignity of it all.

Suddenly, Angelica noticed the forensic team had made their way into the study across the hallway, everyone moving along the large Persian rug to the upright case whose glass door was standing wide open, just the way she and Emanuel had found it. They had made a point not to touch anything. Angelica knew that inside the case there was a missing item in the exact shape of the dagger now sticking out of Peter Castor's chest. The team had already examined the master bedroom and then followed the trail of blood as it led from the large nightstand next to the bed, through the dining room, the living room, and ended in the foyer where the body lay. Angelica overheard the team conversing about the blood spots as they circled and photographed each one individually. The trail was a dead giveaway as to where her father had been stabbed. Anyone could see that her father must have been in his bedroom and that after being stabbed, he staggered through the house on the most direct route to the front, trying to get to the kitchen as, according to the C.S.I. team, all the phone lines had been cut. All except the kitchen wall phone, which Angelica knew was on a separate line. This meant that the killer did not know the house and did not realize the live kitchen phone existed.

Abruptly, Angelica encountered Detective Tracy, who gave her nothing more than a slight nod as he went about examining the doors. Angelica knew there were no broken locks and no signs of forced entry. She and Emanuel had checked that very fact when they returned home from the movies and found their father dead. After examining every way possible into the house, Angelica assumed the detective would further conclude that the killer was inside the house sometime before they returned home and had let himself out through one of the many doors.

Suddenly, this phase of the investigation was over. The C.S.I. team was wrapping up. Fingerprints had been collected (none on the dagger, of course), the blood samples had been catalogued, and the spots photographed, all presumedly to be used as evidence if and when the killer was apprehended. Angelica's thoughts once again gnawed at her. Her father's killer would never be caught. She was certain. She sighed and clung tighter to her brother's arm. She wanted this to be over. She wanted everyone out of their house. All that was left now were the questions the detective would ask. Angelica barely felt her feet as they carried her into one of the sitting rooms. She perched herself on the edge of the sofa cushion beside the others to be questioned. They would each wait their turn. Oh, when would this nightmare end? When would there be peace again? When? But Angelica Castor knew that peace and stability would never again be possible. This night was going to be endless, ever growing and ever changing. And now, it was time for the questioning.

***

The four people turned silently as the detective
entered the room. Angelica and Emanuel were flanked by
their father's personal chef and their longtime housekeeper.
They were all sitting on the red velvet couch, almost side
by side, straight-backed and unsmiling. Angelica felt the
detective's eyes on her when he entered the room, a small
notebook in his right hand. Was this the man who would
solve the case and name the killer? Once again, Angelica
had her doubts, even as he spoke.

"Thank you everyone. The forensic team is done for
now. I'm so sorry for your loss. I know this is a very
difficult time for all of you. But I want to have as much
information as I can so I can apprehend whoever
committed this crime. And for that, I need your help."

The three heads beside Angelica nodded in
agreement. Angelica's did not.

"So, this is the time when you should tell me if you
have any idea who that person might be. Did Mr. Castor
have any enemies? Are there any ex-wives or ex-friends?
Anyone who might want to see the man dead?"

At the word *dead*, Angelica Castor could feel
Emanuel's arm slipping around her shoulder with a move
to bring her in closer to his side. Angelica's brother turned
to Detective Tracy. "We don't know of anyone who would
want to do this to our father, Detective. Absolutely no one."

Angelica felt Detective Tracy's gaze resting on her
as he turned. Was it time for her to supply answers?
Instead, the handsome Detective's question was addressed
to her brother. "Perhaps you could tell me what transpired
here tonight, Mr. Castor. Where did you go, and what time
did you return home?"

Angelica observed, along with everyone else, as Emanuel stood and paced back and forth across the green and white carpet she had purchased at the ABC Store in the Village, an impulse buy that had turned the once drab room into a cheerful and colorful sanctuary. After a moment, he stopped, reached into his pants pocket, and pulled out two movie stubs. He set them on the coffee table.

"Angelica and I went to the movie this evening, Detective. Our father retires early. He was quite asleep when we left the house. We wanted to make the 7:40 movie, so we left here around 7:10. We needed time to park the car and then locate our favorite seats; I like to sit in the fourth or fifth row. The ticket salesman there knows us. We go to the movie every Wednesday night. After the movie, we stopped at a small coffee shop. I will give you the name. They also know us there and can confirm. We came into the house together around 11:00 o'clock. Through the garage door."

Emanuel Castor stopped and indicated the two people on the sofa. "John and Susan here were off duty tonight. They were not present. I called them at John's house right after I called the police. They both came right away."

Angelica observed Detective Tracy making a few notes in his notebook. He then turned back to the four. And, this time, his question was directed her way. "Do you mind if I ask if your mother is still alive, Miss Castor?"

Angelica held her composure. She hid her emotions inside a slight smile. "She is not, Detective. My mother died twenty years ago. Her name was Rosalina Gomez Castor. She was of South American descent. But you know what the green Lady says out there in the harbor about *your huddled masses yearning to breathe free.* That was my mother, part of the huddled masses. She barely knew my father when she married him. It was a marriage of convenience. For both."

"And since your mother's death, did your father have any disgruntled exes or girlfriends?"

"Yes. There is Selma Ramirez. As you will soon find out, my father always seemed to gravitate toward women with Latin blood who just happened to need money. To prove my point, Father put this Selma in his will when they were on what he thought was the brink of marriage. She insisted upon it."

"And where is this Selma Ramirez now? Do you have a phone number and address? And I will need the name of your father's attorney."

Angelica Castor nodded and left the room. She retrieved a piece of paper in her desk she had tucked away for safekeeping. She had a feeling she might need it someday. And that day was here. The paper contained a phone number and an address for Miss Selma Ramirez of Queens. In addition, she pulled out a card belonging to her father's attorney, Mr. William Porter, Esq. Angelica was confident that Mr. Porter would give the detective any information he wanted. There was nothing to hide. Once back inside the sitting room, Angelica handed the detective the information he was seeking and resumed her seat on the couch. She watched Detective Tracy turn next to the cook and the housekeeper.

"Mr. Cruz and Miss Danbury, can you account for your whereabouts this evening?"

After glancing at one another, John Cruz answered for both. "We left the mansion around 6 o'clock, Detective. And we went straight to my house."

"And when you left the mansion, Mr. Peter Castor was alive and well?"

"Yes, sir. I had prepared his meal: filet of sole, new potatoes, spinach almondine, and a piece of chocolate raspberry cake."

"Did Angelica and Emanuel eat with their father?"

"No. They had a sandwich before leaving for the

movie? Tuna, I believe. Right, Angelica?"

Angelica Castor nodded her head. The cook continued without noticing. "After cleaning up, Miss Danbury and I left for my house in my car. We rented a movie at the video store. *Love Story* with Ryan O'Neil and Ali McGraw. We watched the movie after we ordered a pizza that was delivered. The delivery boy knows me. I get tired of my own cooking, so I order out a lot. After the movie, we watched some TV until we received the call from Emanuel. We rushed over as soon as we hung up."

Angelica made a mental note as to what the cook had said while Detective Tracy nodded and turned back to all four.

"Okay, everyone. I am going to have more questions later. But not until I get the autopsy report and establish the time of death. Please do not leave town. In fact, if you wouldn't mind, could all four of you reside in the house? I'm assuming there are more than enough bedrooms. Just until the investigation is underway and I have some answers?"

Angelica didn't like this. All four of them staying here in the mansion? But she went along with the request. No need to rock the boat.

When the interrogation was over and they were dismissed, Angelica left the front room and proceeded to the foyer, following behind Detective Tracy. Her father's body was just being removed. She continued to observe the detective, who was staring at the area outlined in chalk. What was he staring at, she wondered. Interesting. She noticed he looked down at a mark on the floor. A deep mark. Like something had made a gouge in the wood. Why was that so important to the detective? Did it have anything to do with the investigation? It must have, as he asked the police photographer to take a photo of the mark. When that was done, he nodded her way and left the house through the front door. Angelica Castor stared after the detective. And

then back at the mark on the floor. She was beginning to
hate him.

* * *

"Real style is being yourself on purpose."
- S. Boyer

Two days after the murder of her father, Peter
Castor's daughter had situated herself on the couch in the
sitting room that the occupants of the house called "the blue
room" as the wallpaper was cornflower blue with tiny
white flowers. Through the window, Angelica could see
that Detective Tracy was coming towards the front door.
Someone should be there to let him in. Emanuel was at the
funeral parlor making the arrangements for their father's
interment; she could not bring herself to go with him. And
the housekeeper and cook were busy with their household
duties. So, she was elected. She slid off the couch and went
to greet him. "Good morning, Detective. Come in. I'm sure
you have formed some questions in the last few hours."

Detective Tracy, in all his glory, came over the
threshold and stood in the foyer. A rug from the red room
had been placed over the spot where her father had died,
hiding the hideous chalk marks that were still there. No one
in the house knew if they could yet be removed. "I do have
a few questions, Miss Castor. They may be a bit difficult
for you. Maybe we should sit somewhere."

Angelica led the way to the dining room where each
of them sat in a facing chair at the end of the enormous
mahogany table. Once they were settled the detective began
again.

"I have the autopsy report back, Miss Castor. As I
am sure you can guess, the cause of death was massive
internal bleeding caused by the dagger passing through the
heart. From the evidence collected, we concluded that he
was stabbed in the master bedroom and that he made his

124

way towards the kitchen. The blood droplets support that theory. But he died in the foyer before he could go any further."

The detective consulted his ratty notebook with the torn cover. "Did your father take sleeping pills, Miss Castor?"

"Yes, he did, Detective. Frequently."

"Well, that is what is so troubling about the theory I just presented. The coroner found a great deal of barbiturates in your father's system, suggesting he took sleep medication that night. In fact, it was a very heavy dose. Enough to keep him knocked out for quite some time. There were more than a few missing from the medicine vial. It appears he was taking more than the prescription called for?"

"I don't know, Detective. Emanuel and I never asked. My father was quite private about his medicines, and he never shared any of his habits."

"I understand that he had a day worker who stopped by each day and checked his blood pressure, his sugar count, and his general health."

"Yes. Her name is Rebecca. . .Becky Woods. She is with a visiting nurse service. Father's doctor is the one who recommended her. She even taught me how to take care of him in case she was ever sick or couldn't come one day. I can give you her phone number and address. Maybe she knows something about the amount of medication - the sleeping pills."

Angelica wrote the information on a pad in the kitchen and then returned. When she did, she found the detective in the foyer once more. He had rolled back the red rug and was running his fingers over the floor inside the chalk outline. Again. He stood when she walked in.

"Here you go, Detective. The information you wanted, and I'm sorry, but I was wondering why you keep examining the floor?"

"Quite simple, Miss Castor. Other than curiosity about that mark, I am trying to figure out if your father would have been able to walk this far with that amount of medication in his system. The blood trail leads to here, but the blood drops were spaced farther and farther apart, and the last drops were longer and narrower, indicating that your father was running. But I'm not sure that would have been possible. Unless he had developed a tolerance to the drug and needed more and more to get the same effect. Of course, there are other possibilities, most pointing to a strong individual. Only a man would have the strength."

Angelica turned the information over and over in her mind. Maybe this detective was as good as they said. Maybe he would find who murdered her father.

"Okay, Miss Castor. One last question. Do you have any reason to suspect your housekeeper or your cook of killing your father? I realize they were at Mr. Cruz's house when you called, but there was more than enough time to commit the murder and get home before you returned from the movie."

Angelica thought carefully before offering an answer. "No, Detective. I have no reason to suspect Susan or John. They have been loyal employees in this house for over ten years. But lately, they both have mentioned money problems. Of course, who doesn't have money problems at one time or another. I can think of a few others."

* * *

"Trendy is the last stage before tacky."
- R. Zoe

While putting the finishing touches on her outfit for the day, Angelica Castor looked into the full-length mirror. She liked what she saw. A sweet little sweater and pants set that looked expensive because it was. And they fit well. Fit was next to godliness in the fashion couture bible.

Next order of business would be to go down to the kitchen and consult with John Cruz on the menu for the dinner. About 50 people would be attending. Angelica had decided to keep the guest list to family, close friends, a few neighbors, and, of course, Detective Tracy. She had decided that she liked him less and less with each passing day while still believing he would never catch the killer. Would her father have approved of the detective? She knew the Howells would. It seems Mr. and Mrs. H. had called the local precinct and recommended that Detective Tracy should continue with the case until he could discover who had killed their friend and longtime neighbor, insisting that Tracy was the "best."

Angelica made a face at herself in the full-length mirror. Those meddling Howells. Father was right about them. They always stick their nose where it doesn't belong. Of course, maybe the Howells are right. Maybe Detective Tracy really is that good. We shall see.

* * *

The after-funeral dinner was moving along nicely. There was an overflow crowd in the front room with its many chairs and a warm cheery stone fireplace with colorful tiles. Another crowd had gathered in the study, perhaps wanting to feel close to Peter Castor. His stamp was everywhere in the room, including the glass case with the empty spot where an emerald-handled dagger once rested. Talk was flowing as easily as the wine. Halfway through the evening, Angelica gave Emanuel a sign, the one they used since they were kids. The two siblings extracted themselves from the crowd.

"What is it, Ang?" Emanuel asked.

"I don't know. Maybe I'm having one of those anxiety attacks that you read about."

"We've just lost our father. You assisted with his

care when I didn't have the stomach. You nursed him when you needed to. You even drew his blood for Becky. Anyone will tell you this is a natural reaction."

Angelica lowered herself into a nearby chair. "I hope you're right, Em. Did you notice if Detective Tracy was talking to anyone in particular out there? I tried to introduce him around. Do you think he will find Father's killer?"

"Stop stressing, Ang. If you want to worry about something, worry about the local news van driving by the other day. Some nosy reporters, no doubt. An unsolved murder always makes good copy."

Angelica nodded in agreement. She hadn't thought about that. A news team. Not good. "Now, let's get back out there before we are missed. Take plenty of deep breaths and drink lots of water. You know what happens when you get dehydrated."

Angelica Castor rose from her chair and started towards the door. "I will be the perfect hostess - for Father's sake, Em. But I just hope that the killer is not here in the house, lurking around somewhere."

Oh, but they are.

* * *

*"Style is a way to say who you are
without having to speak." - Anonymous*

It had been a few days since the funeral. The investigation seemed to be going as well as to be expected. Detective Tracy had informed Angelica and Emanuel that he had spoken with almost everyone. Briefly. The ex, the lawyer, the banker, the doctor. At the funeral, he had even spoken with Angelica's sometime boyfriend Trent Boyd and Emanuel's fiancé Yevette Lindsey. He would need a more extensive interview of course. Unfortunately, the solution to the murder was no further along than when he had started.

Angelica was not surprised. Earlier in the day, Detective Tracy had called and asked to meet with the four members of the household once again. All had agreed to be present and sit down with the detective. The meeting was to be that evening.

* * *

Angelica watched Detective Tracy pace around the room. He had not looked happy earlier when he arrived for the question-and-answer session. He turned to the housekeeper and the cook. "Ms. Danbury and Mr. Cruz, I confirmed that you were both at Mr. Cruz's house the night Mr. Peter Castor died. And I did this, not as you may have guessed, from the information you provided regarding the pizza delivery boy. No, it seems that you, Miss Danbury, are being followed. Your ex-husband, Richard Danbury, has hired a private investigator to tail you for the past month. Apparently, he believes you and Mr. Cruz are secretly married, and he wants some evidence. I contacted the P.I. and he showed me his sheets for the night in question. You were both at Mr. Cruz's house."

Next, Tracy turned to her. His eyes softening a bit. "Miss Castor, I contacted your boyfriend, Mr. Boyd. He was very helpful, but not at first. I had to reassure him a bit and calm him down. He was quite insulted that I even suspected him. But we came to a mutual agreement; I would ask the questions, he would answer, and then I would go away and never come back. Turns out that's what happened."

Angelica sighed visibly. A relief. She knew, for a fact, Trent Boyd was not a killer.

"So, it seems I am going to need to solve this case with pure physical evidence alone. I'm going back to the forensic team, the precinct photographer, the coroner, and

129

anyone who was here that night, and I am going to rely on that evidence to reconstruct the crime and hope that it's enough. So, I am asking for full cooperation from the four of you. You are living here in the house..."

Angelica interrupted Tracy's narrative before he could continue. "I think I speak for everyone, Detective, when I say you have our full cooperation."

"Thank you, Miss Castor. I hope I won't need to bother you. I will try to keep my team out of your way. But, unfortunately, I may have to revisit everyone involved. I'm sorry."

Angelica Castor smiled. A homicide detective with feelings? Who knew? She was starting to form a crush; sort of a love/hate crush. "Please, Detective, call me Angelica."

* * *

"People will always stare.
Make it worth their while."
- W. Wilson

Angelica came down the stairs just in time to see Becky Woods, her father's day nurse, coming through the front door and into the foyer, which was teeming with forensic workers. Becky waved up to Angelica, who returned the wave, being careful to step over the man who was taking photographs of the lower stairs. At the foot of the staircase, Angelica met up with the day nurse.

"Hello, I didn't know you were being dragged in today, Becky. Did Detective Tracy call you?"

"Yes, don't you love him? Who would ever think a New York City detective could be so articulate? And so kind at the same time. I can't wait to see him in person. Or maybe I saw him at the funeral. There was one guy I didn't recognize. . .oh, please let it be him. Tell me, is he as handsome as I think he is?"

Angelica nodded. "You'll find Detective Tracy in

the study. Oh, and I guess I should ask for the key, now that
we don't need your services. Please let Detective Tracy
know I took it back. I know that you are mentioned in
Father's will. I will compensate you with a day's pay if you
can make the trip into Manhattan."

Becky Woods smiled. "That won't be necessary,
Angelica. I will be there. And now, where can I find this
handsome Detective Tracy?"

Thirty minutes later, Angelica saw Becky Woods
leaving the house. The day nurse flashed a thumbs-up sign
to Angela and then laughed as she walked out the door.
Angelica straightened her shoulders before going down the
hall into the study, where she knew she would find the
charismatic detective. When she entered the room, she
discovered Emanuel was with him, their heads together.
She was surprised.

"Hello, Detective. Brother. . .are you two
collaborating on something important?"

Detective Tracy stepped back and held up his ratty
notebook. "Your brother was just filling in a few blanks for
me, Miss Castor. I have a great interest in Miss Becky
Woods. Emanuel tells me she was here every day and that
she taught you how to draw your father's blood and care
for him on the days she was not. And Miss Woods
informed me that she has given you back the key to this
house. Now, do you have any reason to believe that there
was a falling out?"

Angelica shook her head, her eyes wide with
astonishment. "No, Detective. I don't know of anything. Of
course, Becky sometimes came while Em and I were out of
the house running errands. Like you said, she had her own
key. And there was no set time for her to come each day.
And, as far as any misconduct, I never heard Father
mention any."

Angelica observed Detective Tracy making another
note in his book. *What was this all about? Was he*

suspecting Becky? Emanuel came forward to stand by her as Detective Tracy looked up from his notetaking.

"Who else has a key to the house, Emanuel? Other than you two, the cook and the housekeeper?"

"My fiancé Yevette Lindsey has a key. And Angelica's boyfriend knows where the spare key is inside the porch light. I checked, and that key is still there."

Tracy made a few notes in his book and then changed the subject. "You know, I have wondered from the very beginning: why a dagger when there are so many ways to kill someone? I am sorry to be indelicate. I hope I didn't upset you, Miss Castor." Her face must have said it all. Did Detective Tracy think she was going to pass out? Perhaps she was. "Maybe the significance of the dagger will come up. I am certain there is something there. Why would anyone grab a dagger unless he was trying to make a statement?"

Angelica couldn't resist an observation. "Maybe *he. . .is a she.*"

"Yes, Angelica. You're right. And now I will see you both at the reading of the will. 3 o'clock."

Angelica watched as Tracy excused himself and left the room. She turned to Emanuel wordlessly. *Was this going to be the day that Detective Tracy would give them a name and make an accusation?* Angelica swallowed hard and grabbed once more for her brother's arm.

* * *

"Style is simply a way of saying complicated things." - J. Cocteau

The name William Porter, Esq. was mingled among the other group of names written across the large glass door. Beyond, Angelica could see two secretaries and a receptionist and a double door just behind their stations. When she and Emanuel entered the office, they were

escorted into a large conference room with a mahogany
table and twenty-four chairs. The other interested parties
were already there waiting. John Cruz, the cook. Susan
Danbury, the housekeeper. Rebecca Woods, the day care
worker. Selma Ramirez, the former girlfriend. Detective
Tracy, the investigator. After taking their seats, she and
Emanuel greeted everyone and then held hands, waiting for
Mr. William Porter.

For the most part, the reading of the will was
uneventful. It was exactly as her father had said on many
occasions. The bulk of the estate was to go to her and
Emanuel: the house in the Hamptons, the land holdings, the
property in town, the condo in Florida, and the money left
after taxes. But Angelica did not care about the money. She
was more than happy with the house alone and the
opportunity to live there for many years to come. Her
boyfriend Trent Boyd would be able to move in, if
Emanuel was okay with the arrangement. And she would
go back to Florence for a few months after getting her
affairs in order. Let Emanuel take care of the details. She
would tell him to put the money into her account until she
was home from Italy. She just wanted to move on with her
life, and. . .

"I just wanted to say goodbye, Miss Castor. I have
Mr. Boyd and Miss Lindsey meeting me at the house to
answer a few questions. And I just received a page from
one of the investigators. It seems they found some items
that might explain a few things. Might tell us how the
murder was accomplished. So, I will see you back at the
house."

Angelica watched after Detective Tracy. *Would
there finally be an arrest? And which suspect would be
detained? Selma Ramirez, Becky Woods, John Cruz, Susan
Danbury? Would peace and order could finally be restored
to the house? Maybe.* Angelica looked down at her hands.
They were twisting around and around. Perhaps because

she knew full well that you couldn't count on *maybe*.

* * *

"Let your style be unique, yet identifiable to others." - O. Welles

Angelica Castor waited in the connecting room. She had set up a station on the far wall and was watching through a peephole she and Emanuel had made when they were kids, wanting to spy on their father when he was in his study. The hole was indiscernible from either side, disguised in the busy pattern of the wallpapers. It had always been a fun game. Today, it was a necessity. After a few minutes, her brother joined her. They watched and listened together.

* * *

Trent Boyd sat across the sitting room, his thumbs doing a rotation dance with each other. A nervous habit that Angelica Castor's boyfriend seemed comfortable with. He was a short man of medium build with dark hair and light eyes. Not handsome but considered attractive by the opposite sex.

"Thank you for seeing me again, Mr. Boyd. I may repeat what we discussed previously, but bear with me. You have an alibi for the night of Peter Castor's murder. We discussed it the last time I saw you."

"Yes, sir. I was playing cards at a friend's house. Weekly card game," Trent replied while he reached inside his pants pocket and brought out a piece of paper. He handed the paper to Detective Tracy.

"I came prepared this time, Detective. Here is a list of the men I was playing cards with: their names, their phone numbers, and addresses. The top name is the man whose house where we were playing. Bobby Atkins. Nice

134

guy but a hustler."

"And the other players will vouch for your never leaving the house?"

"I know they will. But I'm sure you will ask them yourself. And as you can see, the Atkins house is in Flushing. Quite a ways from here. It usually takes me over an hour to get there and then back again."

Detective Tracy nodded in agreement.

"I also understand that you came to Mr. Peter Castor for money. And he turned you down."

"Yes, sir. He didn't like me much. I rubbed him the wrong way for some reason."

"What did you need the money for?"

"I have a few debts, Detective. I was hoping to clear my credit and apply for a loan. I am opening my own business soon, and I was counting on Mr. Castor to help me out. I had even worked out a very neat little repayment plan. With interest. But he refused me. Now, you don't think that I. . ."

"I'm not thinking anything, Mr. Boyd. Do you know who might have wanted Peter Castor dead?"

"No, sir. I don't."

"When you first heard he had been murdered, whose name came to your mind?"

"No one. I figured it was probably some intruder. Or a burglary gone wrong. Maybe Mr. Castor surprised the burglar in the study, and the burglar grabbed the dagger out of the case and killed him."

Tracy took on a "and now something serious" look.

"Okay. Please send in Miss Lindsey on your way out, Mr. Boyd."

* * *

Yevette Lindsey was a very shy creature with long dark hair and green eyes. Emanuel Castor's fiancé was pretty in a natural sort of way. It was a sure bet that the girls behind the Bloomingdales make-up counter would have loved to get their hands on this one. But even without lipstick and mascara, the young woman had kind eyes and a warm smile. And she was very helpful.

"Well, Detective, I'm sure you've heard by now that I came to see Mr. Castor a few weeks ago for a favor. Emanuel is. . .did I say is? I meant *was*. He *was* a bit afraid of his father. But I knew he had to have his father's approval before we could get married. This engagement ring has been on my finger for two years. So, I came here and approached Mr. Castor. But he said he couldn't give his approval until I had been checked out thoroughly like he was buying a racehorse who needed vetting. Was he going to check my teeth and my fetlocks? Really! I was insulted, of course. Who wouldn't be? But I left without saying anything that I wouldn't be able to take back later."

Tracy got right to the point. "Tell me, Miss Lindsey, where were you the night of the murder?"

"I was babysitting for my sister. My little nephew is quite a handful, and she needs to get out of the house. Emanuel and Angelica go to the movies on Wednesday nights; everyone knows that. So, I volunteered to help. I got there around six and left about 10:39 pm. I noticed the clock on my way out."

Tracy finished writing in his notebook before turning back to the young woman. "I was wondering if you have any thoughts as to who might have killed your future father-in-law. Is there anyone in the household who might be unhappy with him?"

"Not that I know of, Detective. Is the answer to that question important?"

"Sometimes I don't know if something is important until after I hear the answer, Miss Lindsey. Now, how about the gentleman who just left? Mr. Trent Boyd? I know you have double-dated with him and Angelica on a few occasions. What is your opinion?”

“I don’t care for him much, Detective. I don’t think he is good for Angelica. She seems too nice for him. He kind of gives me the creeps. He hasn’t done anything in particular; it’s just a feeling.”

“Okay, thank you, Miss Lindsey. Here’s my card. If you think of anything else that might be helpful with the investigation, please call me.”

* * *

Angelica and Emanuel backed away from the peepholes that looked directly into their late father’s study and stared at one another. “I think that went well, don’t you, Ang?” Emanuel asked.

“Yes. I agree. Detective Tracy shouldn’t have any reason to suspect either one of them. Although I was a little surprised that Yevette doesn’t like Trent. Why do you suppose she said that?”

Emanuel Castor shrugged his shoulders. “Who knows? You know how sensitive Yevette can be. Maybe Trent said something to offend her.”

Angelica thought for a minute and then shook her head. “Trent doesn’t say offensive things. I really don’t. . .Oh, they’re coming out. Let’s go and meet them in the hallway.”

* * *

“Style. . .is the answer to everything.”
— Anonymous

At the apartment in Queens, Becky Woods let Detective Tracy and Angelica Castor into her front room. When they were seated, she offered tea and coffee. When both declined, she snuggled into one of her chairs and waited. Angelica could see that she was a bit nervous. Her

137

hand shook when she went to stroke her arm. And her feet were tapping randomly.

"What can I do for you, Detective? Something I haven't already done? I was just the day worker."

"I know it's repetitious, Miss Woods, but I've been wondering about a few things since we first talked. Could you tell me again where you were on the night of the murder? And who could corroborate your story? And please be specific."

Angelica could see a few beads of sweat forming on the right side of Becky Woods' forehead despite the cool air coming through the nearby window. "Well, like I've said, I came home from work; I had a client after Mr. Castor, a Mr. Woo over in East Patchogue. Once I was done with Mr. Woo, I came home, took a shower, and then watched a little bit of television. Let's see, it was a Wednesday night so maybe WKRP in Cincinnati and . . ."

"What about around eight o'clock? Did you see anyone, talk to anyone on the phone?"

"No, Detective. I've told you. I was alone. And no phone calls."

Angelica could feel the tension in the room. *What is going on here? No, no, no. This can't be. This is all wrong. Becky Woods is not a killer.* Then Becky Woods surprised her by opening her mouth and blurting out in an uncharacteristic tone of voice. "What is it, Detective? How rude. Why are you looking at me like that?"

"It's simple, Miss Woods. I want to remember the moment that you started telling me the truth. Now, let's start again. Where were you on the night of the murder?"

*"Never let "window dressing" become confused
with real "style" – Anonymous*

Angelica couldn't believe it had gone so wrong at Becky Woods' house. The tension followed her and Detective Tracy out the door and remained in the front seat of the car. Becky Woods had admitted that she had lied about where she was the night of the murder. She hadn't been at home watching television. She had been out. She said she was only shopping in town, but Tracy had questioned her further about why she had felt the need to lie. Becky had not given him a plausible answer but stood firm on the fact that she was only shopping. Not committing murder. Angelica felt ill at ease and uncomfortable as they drove to the next stop. Of course, that could have been because the next person they were visiting was the last person in the world she wanted to see at this moment. But it was too late to back out.

Selma Ramirez lived in a nice neighborhood on the Upper West Side. When Angelica Castor and Detective Tracy arrived, Selma was just putting on some coffee. The house was warm and toasty. Selma greeted Angelica like a long-lost friend, gushing with staged flattery, which made Angelica cringe. Selma then directed the two to seat themselves in the dining room. Angelica sat on a stool at the end of the table while Detective Tracy lowered his frame onto a side chair. Selma was biting at her cuticles and crossing one leg over another, as if anticipating a direct hit. Detective Tracy didn't disappoint.

"I'm here investigating a crime, Miss Ramirez. Mr. Peter Castor's murder. I wonder if you could fill in a timeline for me."

"Of course, Detective. At eight o'clock that night, I was here soaking in the tub upstairs. I had an unusually hard day. Around that time, I was just turning a nice shade of prune."

"And you saw no one the entire night? There is no one to verify your story."

"No."

"Miss Ramirez, would you mind telling me about your relationship with Peter Castor."

Selma looked at Angelica and smiled as if to say, "Is this guy for real?" and then turned back to Tracy. "I'm sure you already know, Detective, but I will spell it out. We were once engaged to be married."

"And it didn't end well?"

"No. It didn't. But I wasn't surprised. I have been over and underestimated my entire life."

"Well, I'm here to ask you if you have any idea who murdered your former fiancée."

"You know, I have always hated conversations in the past tense. But to answer your question, no. I know who *didn't* do it. Angelica and Emanuel. They worshipped their father."

Angelica felt her face turning red as Selma Ramirez turned in her direction. Was she going to have to "thank" the woman who tried to steal their father's money by marrying him on a sham? Well, she wouldn't. She wouldn't. She. . .

Tracy's voice cut through Angelica's thoughts. "Okay, Miss Ramirez. I don't think I have any more questions. But I was wondering. Do you have any idea why someone would use such an unusual weapon?"

"I guess you haven't heard, Detective," Selma Ramirez said with a chuckle. "Seems wine, cheese, and daggers are back in style."

Once back on the street and heading to the car, Detective Tracy addressed Angelica. "What did you think of her responses? You know her. Was she telling the truth?"

"I don't know, Detective. I have never trusted her. I'm sorry, but I'm not a good judge."

When they arrived at the car, Angelica stopped in front of the handsome detective. "So, what did *you* think of her answers?"

Detective Tracy reached over and held the door open as Angelica slipped into the passenger seat of the sedan. He leaned down so he was almost on her level. "I'm not sure, Miss Castor. But one thing is certain. When I asked about her alibi for the night of the murder, she started by saying where she was at 8p.m. I never told her what time the murder took place. It wasn't in the papers or on the news. And, another thing, the media has been reporting that your father was stabbed, but no one has ever mentioned the word dagger."

Angelica swallowed hard and bit her lower lip as Detective Tracy closed her door and went to the driver's side. Once behind the wheel, he gave her a questioning look. He didn't have to ask. "The answer is yes, Detective."

* * *

"To do a dull thing with style is better than doing an exciting thing without it."- C. Bukowski

Angelica Castor closed her eyes and held her breath. This was the moment she had waited for. It had been days and nights of anguish. Sometimes with no sleep. But here it was. Today was the day. Detective Tracy had called and asked everyone involved in the case to assemble in the great house. He had provided Angelica a list of the people he needed to see.

1. Trent Boyd - Angelica's boyfriend
2. Emanuel Castor - Angelica's brother
3. Yevette Lindsey - Emanuel's fiancé
4. Selma Ramirez - Peter Castor's ex-girlfriend

5. Susan Danbury - The housekeeper
6. John Cruz - The cook
7. Becky Woods - The day care worker

And they were all to meet in the foyer at eight pm.
Angelica didn't like the foyer. She avoided it as much as
possible. But sometimes you couldn't avoid something.
And, apparently, a meeting in the foyer was necessary for
Detective Tracy. So, she would go along with his plan. As
long as he announced an arrest, it would all be worth it. An
arrest. Finally.

Angelica asked John to prepare some refreshments
before joining everyone in the foyer. Detective Tracy
arrived soon after they were all assembled, and he had a
police officer with him. Angelica was delighted at the
thought of the officer escorting someone out the door in
handcuffs. Preferably Selma Ramirez. The woman was a
cancer. And she believed that Detective Tracy had seen
through her two faces. In fact, she was sure of it. Selma
Ramirez would pay for the death of Peter Castor.

Detective Tracy's opening remarks were chilling.
They sent shivers down Angelica's spine. "I believe
someone in this room is a murderer. That may be a correct
statement. I hope you all appreciate that this case has not
been an easy one. In fact, it was so difficult that I hesitated
to come here today without good news or an explanation of
which direction the investigation has taken us."

Angelica watched as the detective crossed the foyer
and stood on the spot where her father had died. Detective
Tracy looked from one person to the other collectively,
until he had made eye contact with each and every one of
the people standing only a few feet away. "The night of the
murder there were no broken windows; there were no signs
of forced entry. The killer is someone who had a key to this
house. We have Peter Castor's key ring with his house key
still on it. And that means that it must be one of you. You

are the only other ones who had a key or knew where the spare key was located."

No one protested. No one spoke. They just watched as Detective Tracy ascended the stairs. When he was up on the top landing, he looked down and addressed everyone below. "At first, I thought that Mr. Castor was stabbed in his bedroom and then made his way up these stairs, perhaps trying to find his son and daughter. He was in a state of shock; he might have forgotten that they go to the movies every Wednesday night. And, then when he got here on the first landing, he passed out and fell over the railing, landing in the middle of the foyer. But my team told me this was almost impossible. His body would have shown signs of blunt trauma from the fall. And there were no traces of blood leading up the stairs."

Tracy descended the stairs, until he was once again standing in the foyer, inside the chalk outline. "Was it possible someone had a way to move the victim? With the help of forensics, we found traces of Peter Castor's blood on the back of the wheelchair. But it couldn't be proven that the blood wasn't from an earlier time."

It was Emanuel who asked the question that was on everyone's mind. "Why would the killer want to move my father? If he was stabbed in the bedroom, as of course he was, why would anyone move him?"

Detective Tracy pointed to the gouges on the floor. Everyone leaned forward for a better look. "That first night, I thought that these marks were important to the case. But since then, my team has been able to discern *what* these marks are. They are marks that just happened to be inside the chalk outline of Mr. Peter Castor's body. In other words, they are nothing."

Angelica watched as Emanuel stepped forward and made his way to the marks in question. He ran his fingers over the grooves before speaking. "These could be anything, Detective. A couple of marks made by a vacuum or one of the delivery men. I hardly see the reason you wasted your time trying to find some significance."

Emanuel stood to his full height and looked the detective in the eye. "Do you or do you not have any concrete evidence, Detective?"

"No. I don't, sir."

Angelica could no longer be silent. "Detective, do you know who killed my father or not?"

Detective Tracy turned. "I don't know, Miss Castor. But here are the facts. Peter Castor had a great amount of barbiturates in his system when he was stabbed in his bedroom, in all probability, while sleeping. The question is: would he have been capable of walking and then running from the bedroom to the foyer? If he couldn't, maybe the killer moved him. I don't know why the foyer, and I don't know why the emerald dagger was specifically used and not one of the others, but my gut tells me that is important. There is a reason for that dagger. I don't know how the murderer executed this killing, but I truly believe someone standing here *is* the murderer. And I believe the motive is a simple one: greed. Money. But I cannot prove any of this beyond a reasonable doubt."

On that note, Selma Ramirez grabbed her coat and headed for the door. She called back over her shoulder, addressing the detective. "You call me here to this dreadful house, and for what? For nothing, that's what. I can't believe I haven't heard an apology yet, Detective Tracy." And with that, the door slammed behind Selma Ramirez.

"I'm sorry for her rudeness, Detective," Angelica remarked quietly. "But this whole thing is horrible."

"Yes, Miss Castor. It is horrible. Someone wanted Peter Castor dead. After weeks of searching using the best team at my disposal, I have no proof, no evidence. The killer is going to walk out of here tonight, scot-free. Maybe they already have. But I am not going to stop searching, I promise you."

Angelica Castor looked around the room at each and every individual. This was not what she had wanted to hear. She had wanted an arrest - an end to this nightmare. And from the look on the faces around her, it seemed everyone else was thinking the same thing. But an arrest was not going to happen. . .*ever.*

* * *

EPILOGUE

*"Never sacrifice your style to get even
with someone who has none."*
- Anonymous

Ten Years Later

The interviewee was sitting in the precinct interrogation room. Across the table were two detectives from the NYPD 19th Precinct. The interviewee didn't look worried. One of the detectives, Salvatore Carruchi, was asking the questions. "And so, you are here to tell us how a murder was committed? A murder committed ten years ago?"

The interviewee only nodded.

"And you want Chief Tracy to be present when you tell this little story of yours?"

Once again, a nod.

"Okay, he's on his way. This had better be good. I don't like to waste the Chief's time. He gets cranky when we don't have something concrete so. . ."

At just that moment, the door to the interrogation room opened, and Chief Detective Nicholas Tracy entered the room. The interviewee smiled, in all probability thinking that the man hadn't aged in ten years. He was still as slim and handsome as ever. Those middle-aged ten

pounds had not found their way to his waistline and his hair
had avoided the bathroom sink. The Chief looked the
interviewee in the eyes and a smile of recognition lit up the
handsome face.

"Well, I see we meet again. I remember you. The
Peter Castor case. One of the few unsolved murders of my
career.

The interviewee smiled in response.

"Yes, Detective, or I guess it's Chief now.
Congratulations. So, this is why I am here. I have just
found out that I am ill. I don't have much time to live; I
won't see Christmas. So, I decided I would stop by. I
thought you might like to know how the murder of Peter
Castor was committed. I won't say who did it, of course,
that wouldn't be kosher."

Tracy took a seat next to Detective Carruchi. The
two were touching shoulders at the small table. He could
feel the suspect's hot breath from across the way.

"Okay, you've got our attention. Fire away."

The interviewee began with slow and precise words,
almost as if speech were painful. "The whole murder rested
on the killer giving Mr. Castor an extra dose of his sleeping
medication. You remember that the coroner found a great
deal of barbiturates in Mr. Castor's system."

"So, I knew all of that. Tell me something I didn't
know."

"Okay, Detective. How about this? You had it all
wrong from the very beginning. Peter Castor was not
stabbed in his bedroom as you previously concluded from
the evidence. He was stabbed in the foyer. The blood trail
leading from his bedroom to where he was found. . .was a
plant. The killer planted the blood because they wanted you
to think that Mr. Castor was stabbed in his bedroom in his
night clothes and that he then staggered into the foyer and
collapsed there to die."

The interviewee smiled, showing straight white

teeth tinged with dark spots. Possibly from some harsh medication that comes with terminal illness. Soon they continued. "…Moving the drugged man was simple. With Mr. Castor lying in his bed and heavily dosed the killer merely needed to swing his feet off the side, push him forward onto the wheelchair and then move the chair into the foyer. Once in the foyer, dumping over the chair would have put Mr. Castor into a position where it looked as though he had fallen on his own accord. The whole thing hinged on his being directly below the suspended dagger."

Chief Tracy did a double take. "The dagger was suspended?"

"Yes."

Tracy remembered back to the words of his forensic team members. "There is no way to tell how tall the perp was because there is no degree of angle; the dagger went straight into the body."

Tracy turned to the person across the table. "Are you telling me that the dagger was suspended all the way above the stairs? Well, that does explain one thing that plagued me all along: why the killer selected the dagger with the emerald handle. It was the heaviest one in the case and the only dagger with an eye at the end of the shaft. The opening could be used for stringing something through, like the heavy yarn we found in the basement cupboard. No one gave it a second thought, of course."

The interviewee interrupted Tracy's ramblings. "The killer ran the rope yarn 'round the staircase's railing and banister many times. And then they ran the heavy yarn through the opening in the hilt of the dagger and ran the line across to the other side of the banister and did the same down the other side of the double-sided staircase. The dagger was suspended directly over the foyer, and Peter Castor, in his drugged stupor, was directly below…"

It was Tracy's turn to interrupt. "But why go to all that trouble of suspending the dagger? Why take the chance that someone would find all the yarn on the iron railing, or was the killer still in the house and they removed the yarn? No wait, that doesn't make any sense. If they were there, they wouldn't need to make some elaborate system of yarn, they would have just stabbed Peter Castor."

"You're right, of course, Detective. The killer wasn't in the house when the dagger fell. After several trial runs, the maze of yarn was so perfectly wrapped, that all the killer had to do was light both ends on fire and let the smoldering yarn do the rest. Depending on how much the killer used and how tight the string was wound would determine how long it took before the yarn burned from both ends and the dagger fell. Gravity was going to do its work. And the killer would be far away, with an alibi that was airtight."

Detective Tracy thought back to the alibis. Emanuel and Angelica Castor were at the movies and the café. Verified. The boyfriend of Angelica was at a poker game. Verified. The girlfriend of Emanuel was babysitting her nephew. Verified. The cook and the housekeeper were together at his house. Verified. The day worker was in Queens shopping. Not verified. The ex-girlfriend of the victim was home alone in the bathtub. Not verified.

Suddenly, Detective Carruchi chimed in with a question of his own. "What about burn marks? On the railing? And the left-over string?"

"The string burned up. Almost all of it. The small remaining amount was removed by the killer. Any ash that was left was never noticed by anyone and was swept away by the amount of people in and out of the foyer that night. And the railing was wrought iron. Black wrought iron doesn't burn. There were no burn marks."

Tracy stood and paced back and forth. "I always came back to those marks on the floor, beneath the body. You, obviously, know. What were they?"

"They were made by the previous trial runs. The

knife striking the floor through a dummy used to take the place of the body. It was necessary to do the trial runs from different heights to determine if there was enough force for the dagger to enter the body. The angle had to be perfect. And, of course, the trial run helped the killer ensure that the heavy string would burn up completely and leave no trace."

"What about the blood spots?" Detective Carruchi asked.

The interviewee smiled slightly. Perhaps proud of what they had to say next. "Peter Castor had his blood drawn for a series of tests every week by his day worker. But Becky wasn't the only one to draw his blood. She had taught someone else in the house in case she was ill or unable to work for some reason. So, it was easy to draw an extra vial and save one or two in the freezer. The night of the murder the blood spots were placed, creating a trail, so it appeared that Peter Castor staggered into the foyer on his own. The space between drops was elongated to appear that Castor was moving quickly, urgently, as would have been the case. And the elaborate plan was so that the killer would have an airtight alibi. It would have taken some time for Peter Castor to bleed to death, five to ten minutes. All those extra minutes, the burning of the yarn, the bleeding, it gave the killer what they needed. When the time of Peter Castor's death was established, it would show that the killer was nowhere near the house."

Detective Tracy returned to his seat. He stared across the table. Were these the eyes of a killer? Or were they eyes that were covering for a killer? "I remember an old story about a form of torture that involves suspending a dagger over a prisoner and lighting the end of the rope on fire. The prisoner either confesses before the rope burned through or…"

The interviewee rose from the chair and started for the door of the interrogation room. They stopped a few feet from the threshold without looking back. "You know,

Detective Tracy, there was one question you never bothered to ask: *which one of the Castor siblings was the last one out the door the night of the murder*? And, of course, no one offered the information that Emanuel went into town to get gas before the movie and never came back inside the house when he returned to get his sister. And, before you ask me - yes, the answer is *yes*. You had the right motive all along. Money. Plain and simple. Greed ran in the family, starting with the mother who had married merely for wealth and prestige. All that pretty money. Unfortunately, certain deadly diseases also ran in the female side of the family as well. All the money in the world can't buy good health, can it Detective? What a shame."

Chief Tracy smiled for the first time. "Goodbye, Angelica Castor," he said to the back of the retreating figure that hobbled painfully through the now-open door. There was no response.

THE

HIGH SOCIETY DETECTIVE SERIES

The guest list is exclusive.
The alibis are charming.
The crimes are anything but accidental.

The High Society Detective Series follows a suave, sharp-eyed sleuth through the dark undercurrent of New York's elite— where everyone has something to lose and someone to hide.

ENJOY THE FULL SERIES...
- *The Fourteenth Man at Dinner*
- *Wine, Cheese, and Daggers (Are Back in Style)*
- *The Case of the Wrong Word*

* * *

MORE TITLES COMING SOON
Stay one step ahead of the next crime.

Visit the Amazon Author Page for new releases and updates:
www.amazon.com/author/marilynsporter

ABOUT THE AUTHOR

Marilyn Smith Porter is an American author known for her compelling mystery, suspense, and contemporary fiction. Her novels—including *The High Society Detective Series*, *Last Kiss*, and *Once More*—combine gripping plots with emotional depth and richly drawn characters. Marilyn's stories are filled with intrigue, romance, and unexpected twists that keep readers turning pages late into the night. With a talent for uncovering the extraordinary in everyday moments, she weaves secrets and heart into every story she tells. When she's not writing, Marilyn enjoys traveling, studying history, and discovering the hidden stories woven into real life.